"You're looking for Skizz." Ed's skin felt tight as he said it. The thought had just popped into his brain, and he wasn't sure where it had come from. But as soon as it left his lips, he knew it was true. He could tell by the wild, wary look that flashed in Gaia's eyes, the sudden tightening of the line of her body. The way her hand tensed on the strap of her bag. Her knuckles, he noticed, were grazed and raw.

Then Gaia relaxed. Her face became a careful mask. "I wanted to ask him some questions."

"That's not true," Ed said evenly, looking into Gaia's eyes. "You're looking for Skizz, and it isn't to ask him some questions."

"Well, don't worry about it," Gaia said. She looked around with studied casualness. She shifted her feet. Obviously she wanted him gone.

Ed suddenly felt afraid. Afraid for Gaia.

Afraid *of* Gaia.

Don't miss any books in this thrilling series:

FEARLESS™

#1 Fearless
#2 Sam
#3 Run
#4 Twisted
#5 Kiss
#6 Payback
#7 Rebel
#8 Heat
#9 Blood
#10 Liar
#11 Trust
#12 Killer
#13 Bad
#14 Missing
#15 Tears
#16 Naked
#17 Flee
#18 Love
#19 Twins
#20 Sex
#21 Blind
#22 Alone

Available from SIMON PULSE

FEARLESS™

BLOOD

FRANCINE PASCAL

SIMON PULSE
New York London Toronto Sydney Singapore

First Simon Pulse printing July 2002

SIMON PULSE
An imprint of Simon & Schuster Children's Publishing Division
1230 Avenue of the Americas, New York, NY 10020

Produced by 17th Street Productions,
an Alloy, Inc. company
151 West 26th Street
New York, NY 10001

Printed in the United States of America
10 9 8 7 6 5

ISBN: 0-671-03949-0

To Matthew Weiss

BLOOD

Mary's dead. Maybe if I say it over and over a thousand times, it'll sink in. *Mary's dead.*

I've been sitting in this tub for more than an hour now. I'm shivering and the water's cold, but I can't seem to move. I keep seeing Mary's face. Keep feeling her hair in my hands. There was blood on her teeth.

Mary's dead. I held her tonight as her eyes closed. Her life flowed out onto the cobblestone pavement of Washington Square Park. I saw who did it. I even fought him. Mary's old dealer, Skizz, hired that guy to kill Mary. Which he did, tonight.

Oh God, Mary's really dead. She won't call me tomorrow. I'm shaking and sore and Mary's blood washed off into this bathwater when I stepped in. She won't ever make me wear ridiculous clothes again. Make me go dancing with her. Tell me her

secrets. Listen when I tell her
mine.

What do I do now? Everything I
touch gets destroyed. What does
that mean for Ed? I can't seem to
get out of this tub. I'm curled
up. The porcelain is hard and
cold under my head. I'm shaking.
I don't want to cry, can't cry,
can't make noise. Don't want Ella
to come up here.

Oh God, Mary's dead. Is it too
much for me to have a friend? Is
it too much for me to trust someone? Is it too much for me to be
close to someone?

I need to think. Think this
through. Thinking is better than
screaming. Better than crying.
Better than feeling all this
pain. I can't stand this pain. I
don't want to feel this. I've got
to stop this.

Breathe, breathe, breathe.
Okay.
No more.

I have to find a way to never
feel like this again. Not because

of my mom, or my dad, or Mary, or
anyone. I've got to make sure I
never, never feel this pain
again.

And I've got to make Skizz
pay.

"Was this all life was about? The stronger picking on the weaker? Survival of the fittest?"

too young to die

DAMN. HE ALWAYS FORGOT ABOUT
that chunk of broken
pavement. Ed Fargo swore
under his breath and gave a
sharp jerk to his wheels. He
pulled himself out of the rut,
then rolled around the corner of Perry Street toward

You Might Get Eaten

Gaia's brownstone. His breath puffed out in the frigid
air. January in New York was as dismal as things get.

Ed took in the scene around him. The ugly stamp
of humanity's feet had already taken its toll on the
winter streets. Pristine white snow was now sullen
brown slush. Plowed drifts covered corners and curbs,
creating treacherous mounds of filthy, spit-upon,
dog-pissed-upon ice. Try getting a wheelchair
through it.

"Gotta get snow tires," Ed muttered. As he made
his way up Perry Street, a memory suddenly clamped
over his heart, making him clench his wheels tighter,
blow harder as he breathed. For a few
moments he'd been distracted from the memory by
other things. For a few moments he'd forgotten about
Mary.

Mary was dead.

Part of him still couldn't quite take it in. Didn't
want to. For the past month he and Mary and Gaia
had been a real threesome. They had hung out,

partied, talked. . . . It was the only time Ed had been with people he considered friends since, well, since the accident. *True* friends.

Sure, separate, Mary and Gaia had both been pretty intense. Together the two of them had been compelling, exciting . . . and infuriating. Like when Mary had dared Gaia to make out with Ed just a few nights ago. Given Ed's deeply felt but hidden lust for Gaia, that had been pretty wild. Weird, but wild.

Ed paused and rubbed his chin in the twenty-five-degree air. He realized he'd been smiling. Again he'd forgotten.

Mary was dead, killed the night before last in the park. To Ed, it looked like a years-long major coke addiction had finally caught up to her. She'd died with drugs in her possession. Gaia had been there, speaking to the cops, when Ed had arrived. Too late. He was always too late.

Oh, Mary.

True, once or twice Ed had resented how close Mary and Gaia were becoming. But Mary had been Ed's friend, too. She'd been fun, beautiful, full of enthusiasm and life and humor and outrageousness. She'd been too young to die.

Ed rolled to a stop before Gaia's brownstone. He swallowed, hard. It was freezing out *here*. What would he find in *there*? He reached toward the doorbell, thought better of it, and pulled back his hand to fiddle with the armrest of his chair, his heart pounding.

Why was this so hard?

During this last month Ed had seen Gaia unbend more, smile more, laugh more, show her soft side more than in the whole time he'd known her. It had been due to Mary. Now Mary was wearing a toe tag. How was Gaia going to react? What's more, how was Ed going to make it easier for her to deal? Gaia had refused to come to the door or talk on the phone all day yesterday. Who was to say she would even let Ed say two words to her today?

Ed's watch said eight-twelve. The Village School was opening its battered wood-and-metal doors right now. Thanks to a bunch of snow days, they'd been gypped on winter vacation and had to go back to school early. But there was no doubt Gaia would skip today. Maybe George or Ella had already called her in sick.

The thought of Gaia spending yesterday with just her clueless foster father or bitchy foster mother to console her literally made Ed's stomach turn. Today he wanted to be the one who was there for her, to hold her as she cried, to comfort her as well as he could. Now he would have a chance to protect her, just like she'd always protected him. Maybe it would even be a chance for Gaia and Ed to get closer. `Maybe he would be able to tell her he loved her.` That he wanted to be with her. Yeah, in *that* way.

Ed took a deep breath and tried to clear his head.

Just as his gloved index finger reached out to the bell, the heavy front door opened. Gaia came out.

In a frozen moment Ed searched her face. Gaia looked pale but otherwise . . . fine. Calm. Kind of . . . *normal*. No tearstained cheeks, no swollen eyes, no pain etched on her face. She was dressed for school in an ancient pair of jeans that looked like they had been rescued from a tribe of renegade dust bunnies hiding under her bed. A pale blue, stretched-out turtleneck collar showed at the opening of a worn, electric blue, puffy down ski jacket. The jacket had a hole in it, and feathers were leaking out. Her glorious blond hair hung in `wet, ratlike clumps` around her head. Ed knew it would be frozen solid before she reached the end of the block. Same old Gaia.

"Hey," Gaia said calmly, tucking some wet hair behind one ear. She hitched her messenger bag higher on her shoulder, strode past Ed, and headed down the block.

For a moment Ed was too confused to do anything but stare after her. Mary was dead, right? He hadn't just dreamed it. His wheels spun as he caught up to her. "You're going to school?" he asked, hating how his voice sounded—flabbergasted, childish.

Gaia glanced down at him blankly. "It *is* a school day," she pointed out. "Is there some holiday I don't know about?"

"But—" Ed bumped over a curb that the universal handicapped accessibility codes hadn't caught up with yet.

"But what?" Gaia asked. They swung around a corner as Ed struggled to organize his thoughts into some kind of a coherent sentence.

"I thought you might stay home today," he said carefully as he caught up to her. *Great. Great sentence. You're a genius, Ed.* "I thought you might be upset."

Gaia sniffed and wiped the back of her hand across her nose as he stared up at her expectantly. "What is it with cold air and *snot?*" she asked, just as the light turned green. Ed stopped dead in his tracks. He had to say something, *anything*, that would help him connect with her. He braced himself, waiting for Gaia to realize he'd stopped and turn around.

But Gaia *didn't* stop. She crossed the street and just kept going, never once looking back. Ed's mouth worked open and closed, but nothing came out.

In a matter of seconds she was out of sight.

Ed just stared after her.

"SHIT."

Gaia Moore stared blankly into her locker, wondering what books she should grab before rushing off to class. She was going to be on time today.

I Am Pigboy

If she could just figure out what freaking books she needed.

"Shit, shit, shit."

Gaia's locker was inexplicably grouped with a bunch of freshmen's. Bad luck—freshmen were even worse than seniors. New kids always get stuck with the crappy lockers, Gaia thought angrily as she shuffled a pile of cascading papers, although she guessed she wasn't all that new anymore.

Hard to believe she had lasted since September. Usually the educational system gave up on her after only a month or two. Schools in Manhattan must be a little more hard-edged than any of the other places she had been, Gaia mused.

Hello. Think, Gaia. What classes did she have this morning? She had no idea. Then it dawned on her. Chem lab. She grabbed a thick notebook and two of the less hefty textbooks out of her locker and slammed the door.

The metallic clang of her locker echoed emptily in the hallway. *Damn.* The hallways were already clear, the classroom doors closed, and the huge industrial wall clock ticked loudly above her thawing head. Gaia squeezed a little of the moisture out of her hair, tucked her books under one arm, and strode purposefully down the hall.

Usually Ed would have been here to keep her in check, to make sure she went to class in the first place.

But Gaia hadn't seen him since she'd left him at the corner of Perry, looking completely aghast. Had he made it in okay?

Gaia dismissed the thought almost as quickly as it had come. Ed could take care of himself. And besides, she was done worrying. Gaia Moore had officially made a pact with herself—she was no longer a baby-sitter.

As she loped around the corner, Gaia almost collided with a small knot of seething testosterone clumped against the wall. She stopped short, blue eyes rapidly assessing the scene.

Several large, dumb bozos appeared to be picking on a smaller nerd type. One of the hulks, whose neck measurement probably exceeded his IQ, turned and trained small, piglike eyes on Gaia. She felt his animal glance sweep her from dripping hair to battered Sears construction-worker boots, lingering on her breasts, her long legs. Jerk.

"Gay-uh? That's your name, right?"

Gaia stood rooted to the spot, her eyes narrowed.

"Take a hike, Gay-uh," Pigboy muttered. "This doesn't concern you." He leaned forward, gripping the soft flannel shirt of a kid Gaia didn't recognize. The kid's brown eyes, wide behind glasses, flashed both angry humiliation and mute appeal.

Gaia frowned with irritation and impatience. Was this all life was about? The stronger picking on the weaker? Survival of the fittest?

And if that was the case, wouldn't that put Gaia at the top of the food chain?

"It's Guy-uh," she said. "Let him go."

The biggest guy snorted. "He's not going anywhere, *Guy-uh*. We've got unfinished business with Zack here."

Gaia felt her jaw clench. "Oh, your business is finished."

Pigboy laughed. "Not hardly."

Gaia moved fast, lunging forward and grabbing his left arm with one hand. She pulled it back and to the side, `felt the ligaments stretching taut beneath his skin.` Pigboy let out a sharp, surprised groan and went on tiptoes to relieve the pressure on his arm. It was useless. Pain and shock contorted his face into true ugliness.

"You don't even know what pain is yet," Gaia whispered close to his ear. She hated people like him. Bullies.

Bracing her feet, Gaia bent and drove her shoulder into Pigboy's back, flipping him. He landed with a heavy, sickening thud and lay motionless, staring stupidly at the ceiling, silently trying to draw air into his flattened lungs.

"Who's next?" Gaia asked, straightening and pushing her hair over her shoulder. Her nostrils flared, and her fists curled and uncurled at her sides. A thin thread of excitement snaked through her veins. She was aware that her breath was coming faster, that everything around her had snapped into vivid focus.

One of the guys stepped forward, a cocky grin on his face. How pathetic. Gaia could smell his aftershave. Was it Old Spice?

She took a step to meet him, but ducked back when he suddenly jerked forward under the weight of something, *someone*, that had just landed on his back. Confused, Gaia took another step back and watched the scene with surprise. But surprise quickly turned into awe. The kid, Zack, was clinging for dear life to Jock Two's back, his arms wrapped around his neck, his legs kicking crazily. The scene was so comical that Gaia almost laughed. The jock stumbled back and forth, trying to regain his footing, but Zack now had a firm grip around his collarbone with his left arm, and his right hand had already grabbed a fist full of the guy's hair.

In one huge, powerful movement, the jock reached over the back of his head, grabbed Zack's shirt collar and flipped him onto the ground, grunting as tufts of his hair were pulled out in the process. Gaia didn't hesitate. As the jock straightened up, she moved forward and kicked sideways sharply, her foot angled up. She watched his mouth open in a yelp as her foot connected and popped his kneecap out of the socket. He crumpled to the ground next to Zack, gasping and clutching his leg. The expression on his face took a few moments to translate into nauseating pain. Then he started to moan.

Almost immediately the third jerk leaped into action, trying to tackle Gaia from behind. She ducked instinctively, planted her feet, and felt him land on her back. With one deft movement she uncoiled his hands from around her neck and gave a little shove to send him flying over her. He crashed upside down against the bank of metal lockers. Bright red blood flowed from his nose. Gaia stared at it, transfixed. Why was it that blood was so surprisingly bright, cheerful, shiny? Like Mary's blood. Like her mom's.

She sensed movement behind her and turned to face Pigboy again, who was now struggling to stand up. She lifted a foot, ready to attack, but out of the corner of her eye she saw that Zack had struggled to a standing position and now he limped to Gaia's side. Gaia stared at him in surprise as he raised his fists and glared at Pigboy, his glasses glinting in the fluorescent light of the hallway. Gaia followed his gaze back to Pigboy. He grinned at Zack, mockery written across his face, but when he noticed Gaia balling her fists, he raised his hands in defeat and stumbled backward. Then he did a one-eighty and fled down the hall.

Gaia's breathing slowed as she took in the scene around her. In a moment she had assessed that this scene was pretty much over. She picked up her books, feeling the tension already starting to fade away. *Breathe in, breathe out. Don't look at the blood.*

Zack leaned against the wall, panting. Gaia's gaze swept him and determined he had suffered no serious physical damage.

It was over. Gaia hoped the guys would be gone before a teacher or another student found them lying in the hall. But even if they were discovered in their current, pitiful condition, she doubted they would ever point the finger at her. She was, to these assholes at least, just a skinny, blond *girl*.

"Wow. That was, uh, incredible. We were . . . incredible, huh? You're . . . Wow . . . Thanks for . . ."

Gaia shifted her attention back to Zack. "Uh-huh," she said, turning her back and striding down the hall toward chem lab. She at least wanted to make it to her desk before her legs gave out.

Even though this always happened, still, Gaia never got used to it and always hated it. During a confrontation, a fight, she was unstoppable—iron and poetry in one freakish, muscle-bound body. But afterward, when danger had passed, her body took a little breather, and she literally couldn't stand up.

Gaia hurriedly ducked into class with a murmured apology to her teacher, Mr. Fowler. A wish flashed through her mind as she sank into her seat—that she could have protected Mary in the same way. She wouldn't make the same mistake again. Skizz had succeeded in killing Mary because Gaia hadn't taken care of him when she should have. She had beaten him almost to death just days ago. But sentimentality, some warped sense of right and wrong, had prevented her from finishing what she'd started. And Skizz had retaliated, but by going after Mary, not Gaia.

Now Gaia would have to go after *him*.

Time to Blow Sam's Mind

HEATHER GANNIS EXPERTLY SLID HER long, silky, shiny dark hair over her shoulder and shifted her weight in her seat. In the desk next to her Melanie was picking at her split ends behind her textbook. Typical chem lab activity.

"Okay, class, what happens if I take the potassium nitrate and add it to its inverse?" Mr. Fowler asked from the front of the classroom.

"You pass out from the fumes and we get out of class early?" Melanie whispered. Heather grinned with a careful mixture of amusement and detached boredom.

17

The classroom door opened, and Gaia Moore slunk into her seat, two rows over and one back from Heather. Involuntarily Heather's stomach clenched, her knuckles slowly turning white on her ballpoint pen.

Melanie's brown eyes focused on Gaia. "What is she doing here today?" she whispered.

"I know." Heather nodded. "Mary Moss was killed two days ago," she said softly. "You'd think that Xena, Warrior Bitchtress, would miss a few days of school."

Melanie smiled appreciatively. "You'd think," she agreed.

But no, Heather thought bitterly, *here she is. Looking as usual as if she slept in her Goodwill clothes.*

A loud thump suddenly echoed from behind the two girls, and they both turned to see where it had come from. Gaia's head was now slumped down on her desk. How rude.

Melanie swallowed a delicate snort.

Heather smiled again. Thank God for people like Melanie. People who adored her. People who agreed that Gaia was a complete loser.

Ducking her head so Mr. Fowler couldn't see her lips moving, Melanie went on. "You know, I can't believe that anyone could like her, anyway. But Mary seemed to. Now Mary's dead, and Gaia doesn't even look upset. What a bitch."

Heather nodded quietly. She completely agreed with Melanie, but right now she wasn't in the mood for gossip. She settled back, letting a studious look come over her face. Gaia Moore, girl loser. Ever since Gaia had shown up last September, Heather's life had taken a decided turn for the worse. In fact, until last September just about the only really awful thing that had ever happened to Heather had been her boyfriend Ed's accident, leaving him wheelchair bound. Heather shook her head. That was past history. A rough time. She was just thankful that she and Ed, after all this time, could still be friends. But why was a great guy like Ed also friends with that bitch? It didn't make sense.

Since Gaia had come here, Heather, the most popular girl in school, had been stabbed and almost died, had lost a good friend, had been burned with hot coffee, had been picked on and teased, and had practically broken up with Sam.

Oh God. Sam Moon. A photo montage, complete with corny, tinkly French music, began to play in Heather's brain. Sam, sitting at an outdoor table at Dojo's, eating a huge plate of french fries. The day he had bought her a Celtic love knot pin from a street stand in Soho. Sam, unbuttoning her shirt, breathing soft against her cheek. Heather's eyes drifted closed as Mr. Fowler droned on about the false distinction between organic and inorganic substances, blah, blah, blah.

Heather and Sam had been going out for nine

months now, and the last four months had been really iffy. They had been filled with anger, jealousy, hurt, infidelity. But mostly they had been filled with Gaia Moore. Gaia talking with Sam, Gaia appearing in Sam's dorm room, Gaia distracting Sam, invading their lives. But Heather wasn't the type to lose without a fight. It was time for her and Sam to get back on track. Time for Heather to reclaim her hold on him and put Gaia out of his thoughts forever. After all, she was Heather Gannis. If she couldn't hold on to a boyfriend, who could? Yes, it was time to unsheathe her claws. Time to blow Sam's mind. Heather smiled.

"What?" Melanie whispered.

Heather snapped her mind back to chem lab and noticed her friend looking at her expectantly. The same way *most* of her friends looked at her *most* of the time.

"Oh, nothing," she said.

So I've been trying to come up
with a snappy reply to all the
"I'm so sorrys" I've been getting
about Mary. Today at school was
pretty lame. Most of those assholes didn't even know Mary,
except from seeing her at par-
ties. They didn't know
her favorite band (Fearless), her
favorite color (fuschia), her
favorite food (sate). Most of
them don't know me either, except
by my reputation as a social out-
cast. So why are they all of a
sudden acting like I matter? Why
do they even care? All day, during class, after class, I felt
their eyes boring holes into me.

   When they don't know anything
about me.
   You know, I never even told
Mary I was proud of her for kicking coke. I never told her how
being her friend changed my life.
Now I can't.
   I can't tell her that she
taught me how to have fun. I
can't tell her how she taught me

to actually *be* a friend.

Not that it matters now. I'm
through with that. The Mary
thing. And the friend thing. Ed
doesn't get it yet. But he will.
He'll have to. It's not that I
don't want to be there for him.
But I can't. I've got to start
looking out for me. Just me.

There are a few things I need
to take care of first. One in
particular. But once that's done,
it's all about Gaia.

Sounds selfish, right?

Well, I *am* my father's daughter.

Gaia alone was perfect. Gaia alone was worthy—worthy of **no** her background, **real** her training, her surveillance. **gaia** Worthy of his attention.

SLITHER. CROSS. SLITHER. ELLA
loved the sound her thigh-high
stockings made when she crossed
and uncrossed her legs. Sort of slippery and grippy all at the same time.

"Really?" Loki turned to face her,
his back characteristically against
the anonymous white wall of this
apartment. At first Ella had been surprised that Loki
had chosen a doorman building for this month's pied-
à-terre. Then she realized that the heavy-jowled
gorilla in the cheesy maroon uniform
downstairs was no doubt on Loki's payroll.

Ella shrugged, crossed her legs again, and felt a
frisson of pleasure and irritation tingling at the base of
her spine. "What can I tell you? You offed her friend,
right in front of her. But she hasn't been crying, hasn't
been doing anything. As a matter of fact," Ella said
thoughtfully, examining one inch-long spiky finger-
nail, "she's been slightly less awful, actually. At least
she's coming home for meals. So old George isn't quite
as twitchy about her as he usually is."

The force of Loki's intense look made Ella's cheeks
heat. Damn him. Even after years he could do this to
her. Blurred images flitted through her mind of Loki
in bed with her, Loki sliding next to her, the cords in
his neck tightening as he moved. Ella warmed at the
memory of his surgical precision, his superhuman

control. His skin was smooth, his hair like heavy silk. There had been a painful exhilaration on Ella's part when they had first become lovers—the young, stupid, beautiful Ella she had been then. Loki was so dangerous, so frightening, so powerful. Yet he had chosen her. Giving in to him had been as strong and as addicting as jumping off a cliff. Now of course she realized that Loki choosing her to be his lover was like Loki choosing Puffs to be his tissue brand of choice. Her stomach tightened. The older, wiser, still beautiful Ella she was today awaited his next question.

"Has she been with her other friends?" came his soft voice. "The wheelchair guy? Ed? Anyone from school? Anyone . . . else?"

Like Sam Moon, you mean? Ella thought sarcastically. She had to gulp hard to keep a jackal's grin off her face. Sam Moon had been *delicious*. Not only had he been fabulous in bed—strong, uncomplicated, and enthusiastic, with the stamina of a Mack truck—but there had been an added layer of pleasure in knowing that Ella was sleeping with the object of Gaia's affection. She almost laughed out loud right now, just thinking about it. Gaia had been eating her guts out over Sam Moon for months. And Ella had bagged him first. It was almost faith restoring.

On the surface Ella shook her head no, trying to look attentive and professional.

"No. She just doesn't seem interested. The only

time I've seen her evince the slightest bit of excitement was when she beat up those kids at her school. Gaia has the emotional capacity of a hyena," Ella said.

Loki regarded Ella coldly. "She's a survivor. Like a hyena, you could put her down almost anywhere, and she would survive. She would adapt. She is very strong, our Gaia."

A tiny muscle twitched in Ella's smoothly made-up cheek. God, she hated that bitch. To hear Loki salivating over her was perfectly nauseating.

"Uh-huh," Ella said, trying to keep the sullenness out of her voice. Jesus, how long was this going to go on? How long was she going to be stuck here, playing baby-sitter to her foster daughter? Daughter. When the very name Gaia made a taste like cigarette ashes rise into Ella's mouth. She swallowed, making a face.

LOKI TURNED HIS BACK TO ELLA AND strode over to the windows. It was already dark at four-thirty. From these windows he could see the big X formed by Broadway and Seventh Avenue as they crossed and reversed positions. He sighed. Ella was rapidly reaching the limits of her usefulness. The open hatred on her face when she spoke of Gaia was more than annoying. Still, he knew Ella was under control. She wouldn't dare touch a golden hair on that beautiful head.

Loki sighed again, this time with pleasure. In the window's reflection he could see Ella behind him, no longer even bothering to pretend to pay attention to him. The woman looked at her nails, crossed and uncrossed her legs, yawned, gazed at the ceiling. The fact that she failed to be inspired by Gaia was proof of her own inadequacy.

Gaia alone was perfect. Gaia alone was worthy—worthy of her background, her training, her surveillance. Worthy of his attention. Worthy of something more than attention. The fact that Gaia had witnessed the death of one of the pathetic props in her difficult life—had witnessed it and not crumpled, had watched her friend die and yet shown no signs of weakness or trivial human emotion in the days following—well, that just proved how very special his beloved niece was.

A thrill of excitement made his breath come a fraction of a second faster. Gaia was more to him than just a niece. As his identical twin's daughter, she shared his DNA. She was made out of the very same stuff as he was. It was one more reason to believe her potential was limitless.

Loki had been observing Gaia for quite a while. He

had been patient, though sometimes a little cruel. In that time, and especially during the last few months, he had been disappointed by Gaia's obvious similarities to her father: her sentimentality, her sensitivity. It undermined her strength, her ability to dominate those around her.

But maybe the time had finally come. Maybe Gaia had finally left that childishness behind with the death of her friend. It certainly looked that way.

Soon the chrysalis would split apart. Soon the beautiful butterfly would emerge. Soon Gaia would come and sit by his right hand as his successor—and his equal.

"WHAT IS CHICKEN POTPIE, ANYway?" Ed asked, shoveling a small forkful of it into his mouth. He glanced across the school cafeteria table at Gaia. Day three after Mary's death and the silence was nerve-racking. Gaia was still showing no signs of weakening or needing comfort. She must really be keeping it bottled up inside.

Why Is It Made Out of Meat?

"What's a chicken pot? Like a pot just to make chicken in? Where do they get these names?"

Gaia looked up at him and almost smiled. That is, her lips pressed together in a flat line for a moment. Which was the most he'd gotten out of her, besides her snot comment, in three days.

She shrugged. "You didn't have to make it, you don't have to clean it up, so what are you crying about?" She took a bite of her own lunch.

Ed opened his mouth to protest, his temper flaring. What was Gaia's problem? Did she think she was the only one who'd lost Mary? He laid his hands flat on the table, but the thought of Mary took the wind out of his sails. He hung his head and stared down at his lunch, defeated.

Ed and Gaia usually had lunch together, though not in the school cafeteria. They were both big believers in searching for lunch cuisine elsewhere, off campus. They had so many places to choose from. So there was no reason to be sitting here in the cafeteria eating chicken pot . . . whatever . . . when Ed didn't believe for a second that an actual chicken had gotten anywhere near the school kitchen.

Except that Gaia had shrugged when he suggested different dining options. Now Ed stared at her, gathering the strength to give talking another try. He was that kind of guy.

"You know, I'm glad you're not a vegetarian," he

said, trying to sound cheery and casual and failing miserably. "I don't get the whole vegetarian thing. I mean, if we're not supposed to eat animals, why are they made out of meat?"

Not one of his most original lines, and Ed had forgotten what comedian had said it first. Still, even though it was the Ed Fargo entertainment hour, he wasn't getting any reaction.

"So, got any plans later?" Ed tried again. "Want to come over tonight and watch a movie or something?"

True, Gaia had only been to Ed's house once before, despite four months of being friends. Just thinking about Gaia seeing his folks again made Ed wish he had kept his mouth shut. His parents, the lovely and charming Mr. and Mrs. Fargo. The ones who were gearing up for his older sister's engagement party. The ones who were pulling out all the stops for her. The ones who couldn't help wincing every time his wheelchair bumped a piece of furniture.

He started to say forget about it, but then Gaia met his eyes. Clear blue eyes, as untroubled as a spring morning in Maine. "No, thanks," she said. "I've got some stuff to do at home."

Ed hated the way her focus slid past him, as if he wasn't even there. This really had to stop. "Look, Gaia. I know how upset you are about Mary," he said, just jumping right in. "And I miss her, too," he continued, watching Gaia's jaw tighten. "Mary was terrific; she was a good friend. It's really horrible what happened to her."

Gaia swallowed and put down her fork. "I don't want to talk about it," she said stiffly.

"I know," Ed said, really gearing up now. "In three days you haven't mentioned her name. I mean, *I'm* all torn up about it. She was a good friend of mine. You guys were even closer." He lowered his voice and leaned across the Formica-topped table. "Mary's gone, and it sucks. We've lost a good friend. Can't we talk about it?" Ed felt upset and uncomfortable, and he was aware that he was walking a fine line with Gaia.

Gaia slowly shook her head, her eyes large and solemn. Her face looked stony and pale, and Ed hated making her feel this way by forcing the issue. But didn't she know that if she kept it all bottled up, one day she would just explode?

He tried again. "Gaia—I know it's not the same thing. But after my accident, I was a mess. I was going through every kind of therapy, and I just wanted to die." It seemed wretched and stupid to be confiding in her this way right in the middle of the school cafeteria. But he had to get through to her. "I was keeping everything inside, too—didn't want to upset my folks any more than they already were. And I figured I wasn't going to stick around long enough to worry about having a healthy mental attitude."

31

Across the table Gaia remained silent. These were things he'd never told anyone, and he felt like he was burdening her. "Anyway," he pressed on, "finally I decided to get over myself. Do the best I could. Part of that was just talking about things. Getting it out. The only person *I* had to talk to was the shrink my parents forced on me. But even he was better than nothing. And you have someone—you have *me*. I just—I don't know. I just wish you would talk to me about Mary. I mean, you—it's like Mary never existed or something."

Quietly Gaia sat there, her breathing shallow, her eyes wide and unreadable as she scanned the room, not looking at him. Ed felt his fists clench in frustration.

How freaking typical. In the four months he had known Gaia, he had seen her furious, violent, shy, antisocial, rude, sensitive, generous, forgiving, and reckless. He didn't think he had ever seen her truly happy, and he knew he had never seen her weak. Why was he expecting something different now, just because her other best friend had been murdered in front of her only three days ago?

Abruptly Ed pushed his lunch tray away. What was this stuff-to-do-at-home shit? Gaia didn't consider the Nivens' house her *home*. She'd never referred to it that way before. Also, if memory served, and Ed thought it did, then Gaia was usually desperate to get out of the

Nivens', and stay out, for as many hours of the day as possible.

Light dawned, and Ed suddenly softened. He leaned across the table, his eyes narrowing. "Who are you, and what have you done with the real Gaia?"

It was an old joke, an ancient joke, but still chuckle worthy, in Ed's opinion.

Instead Gaia looked suddenly, inexpressibly sad. It was only for a moment, but sadness washed over Gaia's face as if she had stepped in front of a tall building that blocked her face from the sun. Then it was gone. Her face twitched back into its beautiful, expressionless mask. "There is no real Gaia," she said softly.

It's Almost Funny

GAIA STEPPED OFF THE NUMBER-SIX local on Eighty-sixth Street and started walking west. The January cold whistled down the wind tunnels made by buildings on either side of her. It whipped her hair around beneath the sweatshirt hood that stuck up from beneath her ski jacket.

It hadn't been easy, ditching Ed. First

he'd asked her to come over to his place. Then he had suggested eating together, or catching a movie, or going for coffee. Was he ever going to get off her back?

Now, reaching Fifth Avenue, Gaia turned left, then crossed the wide street, heading for the huge columns of the Metropolitan Museum of Art. Here was the plan: first, an hour of culture, then a bowl of potato-leek soup from the soup Nazi, then a couple of hours downtown in and around Washington Square Park and Tompkins Square Park, enjoying the lovely January weather and looking for her good old pal Skizz under cover of darkness.

Gaia shivered in anticipation. Never once had she considered using her unique strengths to take another person's life. Now she could think of nothing else.

A mental movie had been running through Gaia's head constantly since the day after Mary's death. The scenes often changed, but the theme was always the same—Skizz lying at her feet; Skizz, dangling limp and silent as her hands clasped his neck; Skizz dead, done, gone forever.

Gaia now rubbed her eyes to clear the image as she climbed the steps to the Met. She knew part of her, a huge part of her, didn't want to kill Skizz at all. Somewhere deep down, a voice raged at the pure *wrongness* of it. How could she take a life? What would her father think? But then, she reminded herself, what did she care about what he thought?

But Skizz needed to die. And Gaia was *past* caring about right or wrong. Was it right that Mary would be lying underground in a matter of days?

No. It was time that Gaia forgot about her silly ideals. The plan was simple—kill Skizz, get the hell out of here, and begin a new life somewhere. Somewhere where no one would know her.

When Gaia walked through the huge, heavy bronze doors of the museum, a strong, heated blast of air whooshed down on her. It instantly dried the snowflakes clinging to her hair. Inside, it was stuffy, overheated, and dry. Gaia shrugged out of the puffy ski jacket and tied its floppy arms around her waist. She snagged a map from the info desk and made her way to a bank of elevators.

An elevator, a couple of long halls, and a wide stairway later, she found herself in a series of rooms devoted to German expressionists. As Gaia wandered over in front of a Nolde painting, she had a flashback of her mother, Katia. Katia had taught Gaia how to look at art, how to love it, how to let it get inside her. She sank down on a bare wooden bench.

This painting was called *Three Russians,* and it showed two men and a woman all bundled up, as if perhaps they had just strolled down a New York street in the middle of January. The brush strokes were coarse and broad; the paint clung `thickly, stickily` to the canvas in crusty swaths. Three

Russians. All dressed in fur. They had long, thin noses, high cheekbones . . .

Katia Moore had been Russian. She had spoken with rolling *r*s and worn clothes she had brought from Europe. She had often had long conversations with Gaia in her native tongue, and for years Gaia had thought of it as their own secret language. Katia had been so unlike other kids' mothers. Gaia's whole family had been so unlike everyone else's. Which was why she was here now, seventeen years old, a genetic freak made much worse by her father's intensive, relentless training. Training that had ended as abruptly as her mother's life, and on the same night. Five years ago.

Gaia's breath lightly left her lungs as she felt herself sink onto the hard bench. It was so hot in here, so dry.

I'm a freak, thought Gaia. *Genetically incapable of feeling fear. Why?* she screamed silently. Why had she been made like this? As a child, when she realized, she *knew* that she simply never felt fear, it hadn't been a big deal. Lots of kids had seemed reckless and fearless—like that day she and four of her friends climbed up to the roof of the Rosenblitts' shed, jumped from there to the roof of the Stapletons' garage, then crossed over to the other side and leaped seven feet down into a pile of compost. Paratroopers! Okay, it had been disgusting, landing in all the fruit rinds and eggshells, but it hadn't been scary. Not for any of them. It had been fun.

But now, at seventeen, never feeling fear had become a weight around her neck. It had made her friends a target on more than one occasion. It had gotten Mary killed. But it would also make it possible for her to kill Mary's killer, with nothing to hold her back.

Standing up, Gaia realized she was hungry. Maybe it was time to hit the soup wagon. She took one last quick look around the German expressionists. Gotta hand it to them—they were masters at depicting all the agonies of the human condition. Thwarted love, psychic torture, the sheer pain of existence all laid out for the viewer in bright, jewel-like colors. All these paintings of anguish. It was almost funny. Gaia hiked up her messenger bag, turned, and left the *Three Russians* behind.

Nothing of Katia

TOM MOORE STOOD IN THE SHADOWS near the door of the Metropolitan Museum of Art. George was right. In the past five years Tom had seen Gaia only a handful of times, and always at a distance. It was simply too dangerous for them to meet face-to-face. It had always seemed like the best thing to do, for Gaia's safety. Now Tom was wondering if he had inadvertently destroyed Gaia in a way that was more devastating than just a physical death. He was wondering if he had destroyed her soul.

The night Katia had died, Tom's only thought was to save his and Katia's child. So he had left, and used his CIA connections to arrange for Gaia to be sent away, to keep changing addresses, to keep on the move. He'd thought he was protecting her. Now it looked like he was setting her up to become emotionally warped, unable to respond to another human being. Stunted. For all of her many and amazing talents, strengths, and resources, his beautiful daughter seemed unable to honestly grieve over the death of her closest girlfriend. She seemed unable to reach out to others for help. She seemed unable to express any kind of emotion at all.

It was appalling, what Gaia was becoming. A month ago Tom had been filled with hope. To the best of his knowledge, Gaia had made some friends, was seeing them, talking, laughing. Now one friend was dead, and Gaia was cutting the other friend out as if he were a tumor. She hadn't shed one tear.

Something had to be going on inside Gaia—that much was clear. It just didn't appear to be the *right* something. In this new, automatonlike Gaia, Tom could see nothing of Katia's passion, her fire, her will to live. What he could see was coldness, detachment, anger. And what else? Mercilessness. Where was Katia's gentleness, her generosity, her warmth and affection?

Maybe Tom didn't know his daughter at all. He certainly didn't understand her. A chilling determination was written all over her face—in the set of her jaw, in the distance in her eyes. It reminded him of someone—and in a chilling flash Tom realized that that someone was Loki.

What was Gaia capable of?

Tom's head swirled with indecision—he, who was famous for being able to evaluate a complex situation instantly and unerringly make the correct, the only decision, felt at a loss. He had no idea what to do. It was dangerous for him to appear in her life, to intervene in the situation he had created for her. It would be dangerous for both of them and for his country. But at this moment Tom felt he would risk everything just to be able to approach his daughter, give her a hug, offer her a shoulder to lean on. Steer her away from whatever it was she was planning to do. But how could he, when the very act of contacting her might be enough to get a bullet put through her head?

Just like Katia.

How can I express my feelings toward my only brother, my identical twin? I can tell you that I hate him, but the word *hate* doesn't really begin to cover the depth of the feeling I have for him. He is light; I am darkness. He is a plodding government worker—I am exquisitely subtle in my work. I have raised what I do to the level of an art. He cannot approach my greatness. Every day that he lives, he taints my own existence. It is clear that he must be destroyed. Only by standing alone can I attain my final destiny.

I have tried to take his life. It proved to be a mistake that put parts of my life beyond repair. For now, trying again is not an option. But there are other ways to destroy a man besides death.

Gaia. Katia's child. She is the perfect revenge. She is the child that should have been mine, would have been mine—will someday

be mine. Gaia is poised on the
brink of greatness. I can see
that now. Before, I thought she
had potential. Now, seeing her
reactions to this latest test,
the death of the girl Mary, I am
convinced Gaia is almost ready to
break free from her father's
influence. She is showing
strength beyond measure. She is
unclouded by emotion. She is free
of sentimentality. She is ready
to be a killer. Gaia will belong
to me.

   And when she does, I will
twist the knowledge of her
betrayal in Tom Moore's heart
like a knife.

Skizz is lying low. I froze my ass off last night going back and forth between Tompkins Square Park and Washington Square Park, looking for him, but after five hours he still hadn't shown his ugly face. But I'll get him. For Mary's sake.

Okay, I know it wasn't actually Skizz who physically killed Mary. The guy I fought in the park that night was someone completely different: someone strong, trained, and lethal. Skizz is a fat, sloppy joke. But I know Skizz hired the guy. I'm not stupid. That guy was probably one of Skizz's clients who owed him, big time. Mary was his way of repaying his debt. The way I figure, Skizz now owes me his life. God knows the police aren't going to do anything to make him pay. To them Mary is just another drug addict who got what she deserved.

After I got back to George's last night, I couldn't sleep. I

thought about all the ways I
could take Skizz apart. Facing
him, sideways, from the back. In
my mind I heard his shoulder snap
as I bent it. I heard the choked
scream of pain rip from his
throat as I broke his fingers.

I also thought about Ed. I
thought about how I never want to
see him again once this thing is
over. I don't want to see the
look in his eyes when he realizes
that I've killed someone. As for
me, I'll probably never look in
the mirror again after it's done
and Skizz is dead. But I don't
know what else to do. I don't
know how else to make it up to
Mary.

He was a
man. A man
had balls.
He would

resolutions

find the
balls to
break up
with
Heather.

NOW, WHY DOESN'T STARBUCKS HAVE

The Nonexcited State

a concession right here? Sam Moon wondered. He stretched and yawned, his heavyweight rugby shirt riding up to expose smooth skin. The life of the premed student. All work and no play. Actually, last semester Sam's life had consisted of too much play, too much obsessing about Gaia, and not enough work. Which his grades had demonstrated. Which had prompted a heartfelt man-to-man with Dad. Which had prompted Sam's starting this semester by working his butt off.

He looked around the study room he was in. A wide wall of glass closed the room off from the central lobby. The NYU library was ten stories tall, with a huge open vertical space in the middle and floor after floor of books encircling it like a vise. It always made him feel nauseated just looking at it.

Sam shifted again. How long had he been sitting here, wading through the text and class notes for his human sexuality class? At least three hours. He needed coffee. He needed a Danish. At the beginning of the year someone had turned him on to onion bagels with scallion cream cheese. He'd thought they were incredible. Until the night he'd thrown one up after doing seven tequila shots in Josh Seidman's dorm room.

Once you throw something up after seven tequila shots, you never want to eat it again. Fact of life.

Human sexuality. What a laugh. The course was required for premeds, and he and his pals thought it would be a hoot. Instead it somehow managed to suck every last bit of humor from the subject and turn it into something so dry that sometimes Sam wondered if the team who wrote the textbook had ever, ever gotten it on *once* in their whole dreary academic lives.

Thinking about sex made Sam think about Heather. Heather was gorgeous. Heather was willing. Heather was sexy. All his friends envied him. But Sam couldn't help it: He wanted Gaia. Tall, beautiful Gaia, who didn't have as much fashion sense in her whole body as Heather had in her pinky. But it didn't matter. His entire being cried out for Gaia.

"Moon Man." One of his suitemates, Mike Suarez, whacked him on the shoulder with a dog-eared copy of *Time* magazine.

Sam jumped. "Hey," he said. "What's up?"

Mike sank down into the chair across from Sam's. He kept his voice down. "You gonna use your meal card tonight?"

The question was so random that Sam couldn't even wrap his mind around it. "Uh . . ."

"I'm broke, lost my card, thought if you had other plans for dinner, I could use your meal card tonight."

Sam fished out his wallet and threw the meal card to Mike. "Take it."

"Whoa, thanks, man. I'm gettin' a new card soon." Mike shuffled to his feet, huge, battered sneakers flapping as he left. He needed to replace the duct tape holding them together. All the snow was making it unravel.

"Yeah, whatever," Sam said. He stood up, stretched again. God, what day was it? Wednesday? Thursday? Had it been only Sunday night, New Year's Eve, that he'd finally had a chance with the object of his obsession? And he had run out on her. He had taken one look at her stepmother and realized she was the same woman he'd slept with the night before.

New Year's Eve. The new year. Resolutions. He had resolved to get better grades this semester. Had resolved never to eat onion bagels with scallion cream cheese. For that matter, he had resolved never to drink tequila shots with Josh again. Maybe he needed to make some resolutions about his warped love life.

For one thing, he should break it off with Heather once and for all. They had little fights, they both cooled down, they drifted back together and back into bed again. Then it would start over.

If he didn't get the balls to really break up with her soon, she probably never would, either. He wasn't blind. He knew it was a big prestige thing for her to have a college boyfriend. And she probably cared for him. If he didn't break up with her, they would just drift along in this lame-ass way, neither of them happy, until finally *boom*. They'd be standing at the altar, pledging to go through with this sitcom for life. He couldn't let that happen. He was a man. A man had balls. He would find the balls to break up with Heather.

Then maybe he could pursue Gaia the way he wanted to: urgently, relentlessly, determinedly. He could wear her down. He knew it. He would overwhelm her with his love. She would soften toward him. Forget his past mistakes. Fall in love with him. And they would be together and stay together. Sam smiled at this image.

Mindlessly his gaze drifted down to the text page before him. It was almost a full-page, head-on photo titled "A Male's Reproductive Organs (the Nonexcited State)." Sam stared at it blankly. *Oh, right,* he thought. *Balls.*

"I'LL GO WITH YOU."

d Bangs His ead Against he Wall

Gaia's eyes narrowed as she looked at Ed. She leaned back enough to shut her locker door, then dropped her bag to the floor so she could put on her ski jacket.

A few limp, grayish feathers leaked out through its hole and fluttered to the ground.

"No, thanks," she said, trying not to sound like a complete bitch and not quite succeeding. "I think I'll just go do it. Mr. MacGregor's on my back about this paper, and I need to knock it out. I can't study on Perry Street—that woman is always on my case about something. A couple of hours at the NYU library ought to do it." Picking up her bag, she slung it over one shoulder and jerked her hair out from beneath the strap.

Ed's wheelchair blocked her way. "What is *with* you?"

Forcing her face to remain calm, Gaia said, "What?" She could see the frustration and uncertainty on his face, and she wished it weren't there. But what could she say to him? *I'm sorry, Ed, but I don't want you to come with me because I will probably get you killed and because I'm going to swing by the park first and if I see Skizz, I plan to kill him, and I don't want you to know that about me?*

"The way you're acting." Ed's arms made choppy movements in the air as he struggled to express himself. "I mean, I need to talk to you, you know? We lost a good friend. I feel like I need some help here, and I want to help you, too. Last night I reached for the phone twice to call Mary to see what was up, then I realized . . . Look, this is a hard time for you—for me, too. But you just keep acting like I should go screw myself."

"I know this is a hard time," Gaia said. "And I'm not telling you to go screw yourself. But I have this paper due. I'm tired of all the teachers getting on my case. I just want to do some stuff, get them off my back. I'm sorry if that's inconveniencing you."

Dark brown eyes bored into her blue ones. "Gaia . . ."

"Gotta go," Gaia said briskly. "Bye." She made a quick pivot around his wheelchair and strode toward the east side entrance of their high school. The one with stairs. The one Ed couldn't follow her out of. She could feel him watching her. It didn't matter. It didn't matter. It didn't matter.

Girl, 17, Slain in Park

"MOON MAN. COME ON." KEON WALTERS gestured toward the tiny black-and-white TV perched on Mike's footlocker. "We're talking national play-offs here."

By squinting, Sam could just make out minuscule football players moving toward each other through the thick snow on the screen. A bent wire coat hanger was stuck into the antenna outlet, and Mike was standing behind it, maneuvering it in tiny increments to get a better picture.

"There! Right there, man," said Keon.

"I can't, guys," Sam said. "I've got to review some of this comparative anatomy stuff."

"Oh, is Heather coming over?" Mike asked innocently. Keon snorted.

"Ooh, Heather, baby," Keon said, scrunching up his lips to make a kissy face.

"Yeah, yeah," said Sam, heading out the door.

He was near the staircase at the end of the hall when a door opened and Sherri Banks stepped out, holding a stack of newspapers. "Oh, hey, Sam. Where you headed?"

"To the library. What about you?" Sam asked, pulling on his jacket.

"I was just running down to the recycling bin. Actually, since it's on your way, would you mind taking these down for me?" Sherri asked, holding out the newspapers.

"Yeah, sure," said Sam, taking them.

"Thanks!" Sherri disappeared behind her door, muffling the sounds of Smash Mouth that had been drifting out behind her.

Sam trotted down the four flights of stairs, then headed to the big recycling bins in a small room off the dorm lobby. He threw Sherri's newspapers into the paper bin. A headline on the top sheet caught his eye.

GIRL, 17, SLAIN IN PARK

Instinctively Sam grabbed the paper and scanned it rapidly. *Oh my God.* Goose bumps tightened the skin on his arms, legs, the back of his neck. "Mary Catherine Moss, age seventeen, was killed on New Year's Eve in Washington Square Park in what was an apparent drug hit," the article read. Sam devoured the details. No suspect as yet; police following leads. Young girl—only witness, tall, blond hair, wishes to remain anonymous—questioned at the scene.

Mary. Gaia. Sam was supposed to go out with them on New Year's. Then he'd shown up at Gaia's, seen Ella Niven, and totally lost it. He'd fled the scene like a frightened rabbit. So Gaia and Mary had gone out without him. And Mary had gotten killed. And Gaia had been there.

Sam reread the article, leaning against the cinder-block wall. *Oh my God.* Mary was dead. Mary had been one of Gaia's best friends, along with Ed Fargo, Heather's ex. Gaia had seen her best friend killed right in front of her! And it was Sam's fault. If he had been with them—if he hadn't stood Gaia up—they might not have been in Washington

Square. Or the killer might have seen Sam and left them alone.

He had to talk to Gaia right away.

"UMPH." GAIA COULDN'T RESTRAIN

the involuntary grunt of pleasure as she bit into her hot German sausage. Only one street cart she knew sold real German sausages, and man, they were

Mugging Is a Big No-no

killer. Well worth a detour anytime, even though it meant getting a bit of a late start on her *Faerie Queene* paper for Mr. MacGregor's Brit lit class.

It was dark now, or as dark as it got in Manhattan, what with streetlights, traffic lights, building lights. Gaia was taking a shortcut down Great Jones Street, heading for the NYU library. The street was cobbled, the sidewalks accessorized by shiny black piles of garbage bags. One really good thing about winter, Gaia mused as she chomped, was that the trash froze, eliminating a lot of the smell.

Taking another bite, Gaia remembered how Mary had introduced her to knishes a few weeks ago. Mary had grown up in Manhattan and was on intimate terms with every street-food vendor around. When Gaia had taken her first bite of a knish smeared with yellow mustard, Mary had laughed at the wondrous expression on her face.

Suddenly Gaia had an instantaneous prickle of awareness. Without even thinking, she quickly stepped away from the curb. The next moment she heard the distinct whir of a bicycle's wheels. Then she felt someone grab her bag and yank, hard. If her preternaturally acute senses hadn't told her to sidestep, this jerk would have knocked her down with his bike. As it was, he was almost pulled off balance as he pulled on her strap.

In an instant all her reflexes were on full alert, her muscles pumped and ready for action. Her right hand clamped around the strap of her bag, hoping it would hold. She gave a sharp pull, and the biker swung in a large, wobbly arc around her, trying to steer, pedal, and pull her bag away at the same time.

Gaia chewed quickly, swallowing bits of sausage.

"Let go!" the biker shouted. "I'll kill you!"

"You idiot," Gaia muttered. Using both hands, she swung her pack out and around, forcing the biker's front wheel to smash against the high stone curb.

He let out a confused yelp, pitching headfirst over the handlebars and onto the sidewalk. Amazingly, he hadn't let go of the bag. Gaia was bent over, the strap pulling heavily through her jacket. She took a big step forward and stomped on the biker's hand, pinning it to the sidewalk.

"This . . . doesn't . . . belong . . . to . . . you," Gaia said slowly and carefully, punctuating her words by leaning on his hand. The biker's face was contorted with pain, and his other hand scrabbled at her ankle, gripping her pants with his fingers.

Bending down, Gaia gave him a `swift uppercut to the nose`, putting enough power in it to snap back his head and make his hand finally release her pack. Stepping back quickly, Gaia straightened and pulled the bag onto her shoulder with both straps. Her breathing had scarcely altered, but her senses were humming: She could smell his stale sweat through his cheap jacket, smell the tangy, coppery scent of the blood trickling from his nose. Bright red blood. The night air felt cold and crisp and seemed to sharpen her vision.

The biker scrambled back to his bike just as Gaia reached it. She anchored her body weight, then spun in a quick, smooth roundhouse kick that knocked him backward onto the sidewalk. He lay there awkwardly for a moment, `like an upended turtle`. By the time he'd crawled to his feet, Gaia had kicked out several spokes on his front wheel.

"You bitch!" he screamed, coming at her again. Almost effortlessly she grabbed his hand and twisted it back, forcing him to his knees.

"Mugging is bad." Gaia's voice, unnaturally steely,

cut through the mugger's cries. "People don't like being mugged. You got it?"

The biker whimpered as she slowly pulled back on his arm. "Got it!" he finally screeched.

Suddenly she let him go. He crumpled to the sidewalk. "You bitch," he croaked.

"You started it," Gaia snapped childishly. She headed down the sidewalk, leaving the mugger behind as she had left Ed behind several hours earlier. She walked quickly, wanting to put as much distance between her and the biker before the familiar lethargy hit her. With great luck, she was almost two blocks away and right in front of a lighted bus stop with a bench when the weakness overwhelmed her, making her knees give out. She sank down on the bench next to an older, bundled-up black woman who gave her a disgusted look. Maybe she thought Gaia was on drugs.

Gaia leaned against the clear Plexiglas bus shelter, feeling all sensation pool in her feet like they weighed a thousand pounds each. A few moments later the bus pulled up and the woman got on, shooting Gaia another angry look. Gaia almost laughed.

After a few minutes Gaia felt the return of nerves, of muscle strength. She mentally checked herself out: All systems were go. The NYU library was just another two blocks to the west, on West Fourth Street, facing Washington Square. Gaia decided to find a library seat where she would have a view of the park through a picture window. Who knew? Maybe she would see Skizz slinking into the park.

Every time she thought of Skizz, an odd trickle of sensation crept up her spine. In her short life she had beaten some losers senseless. She had sometimes even enjoyed the physical and mental challenge that a closely matched fight presented. But this was different. There was no turning back from murder.

Gaia's thoughts turned to the guy who had killed Mary. The one who had actually pulled the trigger. Now, *there* had been a closely matched fight. He had been unusual, Gaia thought as the NYU library loomed ahead of her. Most people she fought were pathetic, unschooled, unskilled—sitting ducks compared to her, with her finely honed reflexes, supernatural strength, years of training, and lightning-fast reaction times. But that guy—he had been different. He had been as good as she was. Maybe better. It was the first time she had met someone like that. Besides her father, that was.

Inside the library Gaia flashed her Village School ID. The guard nodded, bored, and let her through the turnstile. There was a bank of computers in the right-hand reading room. Gaia headed there. The computers had access to both the Internet and the library's card catalog. It would be a good place to start. And the reading room had a view of the park.

In the room bright fluorescent lights made everything look sort of washed out and off register, made the students look even more pasty faced and hollow eyed.

Now Gaia needed a chair that faced the doorway. It was a habit she'd picked up from her father. There was an easy chair with a view of the window, but it was mostly hidden behind a scratched Formica end table with a depressed-looking philodendron on it. Gaia headed toward it, automatically checking out the scene for weird vibes, possible sources of danger, likely escape routes. It was something she did without thinking, almost without being aware of it. Even in an innocuous place like a library.

As she glanced around, she became aware of someone watching her—and a moment later she found herself staring into a pair of beautiful, startled hazel eyes. It took her brain less than a thousandth of a second to register why those eyes looked familiar. They belonged to Sam Moon.

This Is Mrs. Moss

"I'LL GET IT, DARLING," GEORGE Niven called. There was a muffled reply from Ella as George headed into the study to grab the phone.

"Hello?"

"Hello. This is Patricia

Moss," said an unfamiliar voice. "Mary's mother."

George had a sinking feeling. He'd seen the article in the newspaper. He'd only noticed it because of the headline, GIRL, 17, SLAIN IN PARK. Then he'd scanned the paragraph and recognized Mary's name. It was more than strange that Gaia hadn't mentioned anything to him or Ella. His knuckles tightened on the phone. "This is George Niven," he responded. "Gaia's guardian. Let me say that I'm so very sorry about your loss."

A hesitation. "Thank you. This is a very difficult time for us." Her voice broke. "I know Gaia must be extremely upset. I wanted to tell her that if she would like to come be with our family during this time, she's more than welcome."

"Thank you," said George. "I'll be sure to tell her."

"I also have a favor to ask her," continued Mary's mother. "But I'll wait until I speak to her. If you could ask Gaia to call me."

"Of course," said George. "I'll see that she does. Take care, and please let us know if there's anything my wife and I can do to help."

"Thank you," Patricia Moss whispered hoarsely, then hung up.

George replaced the receiver and rubbed his chin thoughtfully. He hadn't seen Gaia much lately. He'd promised Tom to keep closer tabs on her, but agency work kept him away most of the time. When he *had* seen Gaia, he hadn't noticed any signs of grief. Mrs.

Moss had assumed he knew about Mary's death, and he had, but not because of anything Gaia had said. This whole thing was getting so much more complicated than he had expected. He loved Tom Moore like a brother and would do anything for him. He'd jumped at the chance to take Gaia in, shepherd her through her last years of high school. But it was all getting so complex.

The study door swung open, and Ella came in, holding out a cut-glass tumbler full of scotch and water.

"Thank you, darling," said George.

"What's wrong, honey?" Ella asked. She smoothed her fluffy, chartreuse wool sweater down over her full breasts and tugged it down on her waist. Then she curled up on the leather sofa, one leopard-print leg coiled beneath her.

"That was the mother of a friend of Gaia's," said George, taking a sip of his drink. He hid his recoil at its bitter taste. Everything tasted bitter to him these days. Ella, considerable though her charms were, had never been a cook. Last night she had made a risotto that had tasted so awful, she herself hadn't been able to eat it. Still, she'd looked pleased when he'd managed to choke down half a plateful.

"Is everything all right?" Ella's remarkable green eyes opened wide in concern.

"You know that article I showed you in the paper earlier? About Gaia's friend, Mary Moss, being killed on Sunday night?" said George. "Mary's mother wants to talk to Gaia. She knows she must be pretty upset." He looked at his wife to confirm the unstated question.

Carefully arched auburn brows drew delicately together. "Upset?" Ella said musingly. "I haven't really seen it. You know what Gaia's like. But since Sunday— no, I have to say she hasn't seemed upset. Are you sure she knows? Maybe she thinks her friend's just out sick or something."

"Mary's mother seems certain Gaia knows," George said, frowning in concern. "Poor Gaia. She must be keeping it all bottled up inside."

Ella made a *tsk, tsk* sound. "That's dreadful. I feel so sorry for Mrs. Moss. And poor Gaia. No wonder she's been so . . . *difficult* lately."

George nodded. Ella pushed her mane of tangled red curls over her shoulders. She gave him an inviting smile. George felt the quickening of his body. His wife lay back against the leather couch, her hair floating out behind her like sea coral. She held out one slim white hand. He moved toward her.

I am not the type of girl who has to wait around, hoping for the phone to ring. I mean, I never have been. Ever since I was thirteen, guys have been asking me out, and it's always been easy come, easy go. Except for Ed. I really did love him. He was like my soul mate. Until the accident.

The accident changed both of us so much, split us apart. It wasn't like I dumped him just because he couldn't walk anymore. It was so much bigger than that. I mean, I was almost sixteen—I had the whole rest of my life ahead of me. And Ed hated what had happened. He hated himself— the new postaccident self, that is. And it got so he hated me, too.

Which is why I'm psyched about us maybe being friends again now. We went bowling not long ago, and it was so fun. Being with him is easy, uncomplicated, light. Not like being with Sam.

Yeah, Ed's still in a wheelchair. And I can't say he's the
same old guy. He's harder now,
not as sweet or eager to please
me. And there's something else,
too, some other layer to him.
He's not just good-time Shred
anymore. He's a little more than
that now. I don't know how to
explain it.

Maybe he's just older.

He would be
lying there,
flatter
than a
pancake but
still
somehow
looking
good.

not

longing.

not

love.

OKAY, I'M A MODERN WOMAN,
Heather thought. *I can express my needs. Right now I need a boyfriend who adores me.*

The Backup Sister

Heather picked up the receiver and punched in memory dial #1. On the other end the phone in Sam's dorm suite rang and rang. "Pick it up," Heather said softly. "Pick it up. Be there."

Things with Sam had been weird for too long. If she left it up to him, they would just drift along like this forever. It was time to put her Reclaim Sam plan into action.

Last summer things had been so great. She and Sam had had such a good time. They had gone to movies, gone dancing, hung out with friends. They'd slept in the same bed a few times but hadn't had sex. She hadn't been ready then.

Now she was ready. Because when she and Sam were making love, she could forget about everything else for a while. Forget about Gaia, forget about Ed, forget about her family.

"Hello?" a voice answered at the other end of the line.

Heather instantly assessed it as a non-Sam voice.

"Hi. This is Heather," she said.

"Hey, Heather. It's Mike."

"Hi, Mike. Listen, is Sam there?"

"Nope, sorry," said Mike. "He's wearing out the study chairs over at the library. His dad had his hide over Christmas because of his grades."

"Yeah, I know," said Heather. "So he's at the library?"

"Yep. I'll tell him you called, okay?"

"Okay." Heather hung up the phone. So Sam was studying at the library. He wasn't somewhere with someone else. Like Gaia. As soon as the thought intruded, Heather quickly shut it out. God, if only Gaia would disappear. Heather's life would be almost bearable again. For Heather, Gaia's existence was like getting clubbed on the head constantly and still trying to go around and live a normal life.

Hmmm. With Sam unavailable, Heather had to move to plan B: be busy, be popular. Then when Sam called, *she* would be out. Everyone knew that guys always liked girls who seemed a tiny bit out of reach.

Heather scrambled off her bed. Though NYU students were already back at school, her sister Phoebe wasn't due back at SUNY Binghamton for another ten days. It was fun having Phoebe around. She was the coolest, even though she and Heather had had their differences in the past. But Phoebe had been really happy lately and really sweet to Heather. Maybe she'd be into catching an early movie at the Angelika or something. A sisterly thing.

A bathroom connected Heather and Phoebe's bedrooms, and Heather heard the shower water shut off. She gave the door a brief tap and opened it.

"Hey, Feeb, I have a great idea," Heather began.

Phoebe had just stepped out of the shower and was reaching for a fluffy gold towel. It took only moments for Heather's gaze to sweep her sister's body. She blinked as Phoebe quickly wrapped herself in the towel, brushing long, wet strands of hair out of the way.

"Whoa," Heather said without thinking. "You're . . . really skinny."

"Really skinny" didn't begin to describe what Heather had caught a glimpse of. She knew Phoebe had been dieting a lot—an attempt to get rid of the freshman fifteen she'd put on last semester. But until now she'd simply thought Phoebe looked fabulous, model slim in her bulky winter clothes. Naked, Phoebe looked like something else. Heather could see Phoebe's ribs, her hipbones. Phoebe was much too thin.

Phoebe briskly started toweling her hair. "Thanks," she said.

Heather looked closely. Her sister's skin seemed stretched over her facial bones. Her eyes looked deep set, her cheekbones carved and prominent.

Without makeup her sister looked pale, anemic, underfed. With makeup, Heather knew, Phoebe looked stunning.

Bending over, Phoebe combed her hair out with her fingers, then expertly wrapped a towel around her head. One, two, three . . . Heather counted the knobby vertebrae on Phoebe's back.

"Um, do you think maybe you're a tiny bit *too* thin?" Heather asked.

Phoebe stood up and tucked in the towel ends. She smiled at Heather.

"Heath-er," Phoebe said in an older-sister singsong. "I'm not dieting anymore. I'm just watching my weight. Trying not to go overboard. You wouldn't believe how awful it was when I put on all that weight at school. It was like, I couldn't button anything. I was practically a size nine! I'm never going there again, let me tell you."

Phoebe turned away from Heather and went into her own room but didn't start getting dressed. *She's waiting for me to leave her alone,* Heather thought.

"No kidding, Feeb," Heather said, moving into Phoebe's room. "Maybe you don't want to be a size nine. But you don't want to be a size zero, either. I think you could lighten up on the diet, maybe even put on a few pounds."

"Oh, no way," said Phoebe, sounding irritated. "My body is finally the way I want it. No way am I going to

69

sabotage it now." Her eyebrows came together, and she looked at Heather with narrowed eyes. "You know, maybe you're just jealous because I'm where you want to be." Phoebe turned her back on Heather and opened her closet door. "Okay, clear out. I have to get dressed."

It was a dismissal, and Heather cleared out.

SAM'S FIRST THOUGHT ON SEEING

Gaia was that his sheer longing to see her had somehow made her materialize in front of him. He'd tried to call her from the dorm lobby, but Ella had answered, and he'd hung up. He'd decided to head to the library, keep trying to call, and maybe later go over to her house and—this was where the plan got fuzzy. Throw rocks at her window? Lie in wait for her all night? Now here she was, right in front of him, in glorious, living color.

Looking at her, at her beautiful, solemn face, he felt like all of his fantasies had been fulfilled. In that one split second he imagined that yes, Gaia loved him, yes,

Gaia had come to find him, yes, they were going to be together forever, just the two of them. . . .

Then he saw the cold, forbidding look in her eyes, mingled with a flash of surprise and something else? Not longing. Not love. What? He couldn't tell.

As she stood there, seemingly frozen, her deep, ocean blue eyes locked on to his, Sam got up slowly from his chair.

He walked toward her. He didn't think about the boyfriend Ella had told him Gaia had. He didn't remember that Gaia had never acknowledged the gift he had given her—a finely carved wooden chess set in a small red box. He didn't remember that he had sent her e-mails that she never answered.

All he knew was that her best friend had died, that he had let her down, that she must be hurting. That possibly she hated him.

Sam swallowed dryly, forcing himself to remain calm. As he approached her, Gaia turned and headed to a chair over by the window. She set down her black nylon bag. His gaze focused on her strong, beautifully shaped hands. Her knuckles were scraped, and the blood looked fresh.

Sam felt hyperaware, like he and Gaia were suspended together in a time warp. He could hear her unzip her bag. Hear the chair cushion rustle as she sat down. Hear her click open her pen.

He took a couple of deep, calming breaths. "Gaia,"

he said, his voice sounding unnaturally loud in the library's silence.

She froze again, then slowly, deliberately turned her head to gaze up at him.

He steeled himself against the coolness in her expression. "I just found out about Mary," he said in a blunt whisper.

Her delicate brows drew together, and her eyes widened. He saw her swallow, then glance away from him.

"I'm so sorry," he said softly, sinking to a crouch next to her chair. "I didn't know until an hour ago." He shook his head. "I can't even imagine what you're going through. I wish I'd known. I wish I'd been there."

Now she was actively glaring at him.

Sam floundered, not knowing what else to say. *I love you? I'm sorry? I made a huge mistake?*

"Did you . . . was there a service for her?" he asked.

If he didn't know better, he would swear that Gaia had just flinched. But she wasn't a flinchy sort of girl.

"I don't want to talk about it," Gaia said.

Sam held up his hands. "I understand. I know you must be . . . Well, it's a tragic thing to happen. I just can't believe it. And you guys seemed like really good friends."

Gaia's jaw clenched, and Sam felt like he was drowning. If she burst into tears right now, he would sort of know how to deal with it. Hold her close, pat her back, stroke her hair, murmur soothing words. But she was just looking at him steadily, as if he were a microbe. An interesting microbe, perhaps, but a microbe.

Sam took a deep breath and surged forward. "When I first read about Mary in the newspaper and realized what night it was, I was just so shocked," he blathered on. "I feel like it's my fault because I wasn't . . . wasn't there. I've been wanting to talk to you about that, about that night, why I left—I just—I um . . ."

"You think it was *your* fault?" Gaia said. He picked up on the anger in her voice.

"Well, because I was supposed to be with you guys on New Year's," Sam said. "And . . . I'm so sorry I wasn't. I shouldn't have left. Maybe if I hadn't, Mary wouldn't have . . . died."

"So *you* could have stopped it," Gaia said sarcastically. She was keeping her voice down, but people still turned their heads to look at them. "The mighty Sam," Gaia continued. "The wonderful Sam. Everything revolves around Sam."

"I didn't say that," Sam said, feeling defensive. "I just meant—"

"You know, Sam," Gaia interrupted coldly, "I hate to tell you this, but this isn't about *you*. This isn't about how *you're* sorry. How *you* could have prevented it. How everything would be perfect if only *you* were there. The fact is, you *weren't* there. I don't care why. But you weren't, and as far as I'm concerned, it doesn't matter if you're ever there *again*. Now, if you don't mind, I came here to *study!*" She leaned forward and hissed the last word. It felt like a slap in the face, and Sam recoiled.

He started to speak again, but she fixed him with a glare so fierce, his face felt sunburned. Feeling like a total and complete ass, he rose to his feet, backed away from her, and slumped back in his own chair.

That had gone well. He reviewed what he had said, and it seemed not too bad. Gaia had deliberately twisted his words. Okay, she was angry at him. That much was clear. She must be superupset about Mary. Too upset to let him comfort her. Too upset to forgive him for letting her down.

Sam sat, smoldering, in his library chair. Having Gaia ignore him so steadily was like having a weight on his chest. But he wouldn't give her an easy out. He was going to sit right here until he had reviewed his comp anat notes, and if that made her uncomfortable, it was too bad. Maybe she would even relent. Maybe he might possibly get another chance.

Did she remember that one amazing night when he had come home to his dorm room to find her asleep in his bed, wearing only his tank top and a pair of his boxers? Every detail of that night was burned into his memory.

74

Sam shifted uncomfortably in his library chair. *Don't go there,* he warned himself. But it was too late. His lips tingled as he remembered what it had felt like to finally kiss Gaia, hold her tightly, tell her he loved her.

Sam stared blankly at his notebook. Minutes passed. Minutes during which Sam wondered if it was possible to redeem himself in Gaia's eyes. Make her care about him. Make her see how much he cared about her.

In a wild fantasy he thought about running upstairs to the tenth floor of the library and flinging himself through the glass partition. *That* would get her attention. He would plummet down, down, down and land with a satisfying, final splat on the marble tumbling-block pattern of the library floor. He would be lying there, flatter than a pancake but still somehow looking good. Gaia, realizing that nothing mattered but their love, would rush over and kneel by him, holding his hand to her breast while tears slowly seeped out of her beautiful eyes.

"I'm sorry," he would whisper with his last breath. "I'm a dumb-ass, but I love you." No, scratch the dumb-ass part. He would come up with something better. "I didn't mean to be an asshole," or something like that. She would forgive him. She would lean over him, her soft breath fanning his face. Her `soft, full lips` would gently, so gently touch his. . . .

Sam realized he was breathing quickly. His hazel

eyes pulled into focus. *Get a grip.* He licked his lips, glad that his face, which felt hot, was looking downward. Okay, he would let Gaia be furious with him for now. But soon he would get her to forgive him. Right after he broke up with Heather.

WHEELING UP TO GAIA'S FRONT

door, Ed felt his pulse quicken. *Come on, come on,* he urged silently. *Please be home, Gaia. Let me in.* He pressed the doorbell.

It was almost ten. Which was no guarantee that Gaia

Come On, Come On

would be home from the library, if that's where she had really gone. If her guardians, her foster parents, cared where she was and when, Gaia sure didn't let it hamper her. But Ed had thought he would give it one more Boy Scout try. He just had to talk to her, had to get through to her somehow. He knew she was hurting. He was hurting, too. And the only person he really wanted to talk to about it was Gaia. Obviously they should be taking care of each other during this nightmare. So why was Gaia making him do this alone? Why wasn't she coming to him so they could help each other? He had to make her see that she could lean on him. Even if she had to bend down to do it.

George Niven opened the door. "Hello—Ed, is it? What can I do for you? It's kind of late for a school night, isn't it?"

"Yes, I'm sorry about that," said Ed, using his best speaking-to-parents voice. The one that had always worked on the Gannises. "I hope I didn't disturb you." He noted that Mr. Niven was wearing his bathrobe.

"Oh, no, it's okay," said Mr. Niven.

"Is Gaia home?" Ed asked.

A pained expression crossed Mr. Niven's face. "No, Ed, I'm sorry. She hasn't been here since this morning. My wife says she mentioned going to the library, but I'm afraid that Gaia doesn't always leave an itinerary with us." He looked embarrassed, as if he should be doing a better job of keeping tabs on her. *Good luck,* Ed thought cynically.

"Oh, well," he said. Another wasted trip in the freezing night air.

"Listen, Ed," said Mr. Niven. Ed looked up. "Did you know Gaia's friend who was killed? Mary Moss?"

Ed felt a fresh stab of pain. "Yeah. We were good friends."

"I'm sorry. It's a terrible thing," said Mr. Niven. "Is Gaia . . . Does she seem very upset about it?" He looked concerned.

For a moment Ed thought about how Gaia had been ever since Sunday night. "Oh, who knows?" he answered disgustedly. "Sorry to bother you. Good night." He spun on his wheels and headed down the block quickly.

He'd come all this way for nothing. His mom had asked him to run out to the bodega and get a quart of milk and a newspaper. He'd used the opportunity to come way over here to the West Village. The plan was to tell his mom that the store had been out, and he'd had to go up practically to Twelfth Street.

Gaia, where are you? he wailed silently as he headed east on Bleecker Street. *Don't you need a friend? Don't you need* me? *Aren't I the only friend you have?* Rhythmically Ed's hands slapped against the wheels, keeping him moving forward.

Making a split decision, Ed turned at the next corner and began the long, zigzagging route over to West Fourth Street. That would take him to Washington Square Park. He could pass through the park quickly on his way home. He could peek into the library. Maybe Gaia was even *in* the park, having a freezing-cold late night game of chess with Zolov.

Ed was breathing hard when he got to the park. His lungs were burning from pulling in the cold night air again and again. His shoulders were tired, and his hands felt like they were frozen into claws. If his parents knew he was here alone at this time of night, they would kill him. Twice.

Suddenly something ahead of him made Ed stop dead in his tracks. His stomach lurched as his wheelchair jerked forward.

Oh.

The scene was no longer marked by crime scene tape, and the chalk outline where Mary's body had fallen had been erased by people's feet and snow. But on the cobbled pavers, Ed could detect a faint dark stain. Mary's blood.

Ed's breathing quickened as he stared at the mark. Was this all Mary's life amounted to now? A stain on the pavement? His chest constricted at the thought.

Almost simultaneously a light-colored flash caught the corner of his eye. Startled, Ed peered into the darkness of the shadows beneath the trees. There it was again. Moving away from him. A million women in the world had blond hair, but somehow Ed knew instantly who that particular blond head belonged to.

He spun to the right, whipping down the path, and managed to intersect with Gaia just as she was emerging from the trees' shadows onto the path again. They almost collided as Ed yanked his chair to a stop in front of her.

"Hey!" She backed up, startled. "Ed!"

"Gaia, what are you doing here?" Ed demanded

stupidly, momentarily forgetting that he had *expected* to find Gaia here. "I just stopped by your house—they said you were at the library. . . ." His voice trailed off as he took in the conflicting emotions crossing her face. Four months ago he would have said Gaia's two main emotions were impatience and irritation, but he knew her slightly better now. He was seeing confusion and almost—could it be?—embarrassment. Discomfort. She looked away from him, as if thinking of a story to tell him.

"Gaia," Ed said again, this time more deliberately, suspiciously. "What are you really doing out here?"

She faced him defiantly. "I *was* at the library. It's right over there, remember? What are *you* doing here?"

"I went out to get milk for my mom," Ed said. "I went over to your house. I've been worried about you. I've wanted to talk to you. I was almost home," he recited, "when I just found myself coming here." He shrugged. "This is where it happened." For a split second Gaia appeared to soften a little.

"I had no idea seeing this would make me feel this way. I don't know." Ed looked at her, his dark brown eyes meeting her blue ones. "Maybe I somehow *meant* to see it. You know, to help me deal with things. But that's not what *you're* doing here, is it?"

"Why not?" Gaia said.

"Because you look weird," Ed said flatly. "Because you've been *acting* weird."

"Thanks," Gaia said snidely. "I already said I was at the library. I decided to hang out here for a while and get some fresh air on my way back to Perry Street."

Ed's brain started humming. Obviously Washington Square Park was on the way between the NYU library and Gaia's brownstone. But he knew she was lying. During the time he had known her, she had *always* been evasive and tight-lipped. But as far as he knew, she had never lied to him before. This was a first.

Gaia shifted her weight from foot to foot as she stood in front of him. She grew visibly impatient. "Well, gotta go," she said, turning.

"Wait!" Ed's voice came out louder than he intended. "I know what you're doing here."

She turned as gracefully as a gazelle wearing construction boots. "Oh, really?"

"You're looking for Skizz." Ed's skin felt tight as he said it. The thought had just popped into his brain, and he wasn't sure where it had come from. But as soon as it left his lips, he knew it was true. He could tell by the wild, wary look that flashed in Gaia's eyes, the sudden tightening of the line of her body. The way her hand tensed on the strap of her bag. Her knuckles, he noticed, were grazed and raw.

Then Gaia relaxed. Her face became a careful mask. "I wanted to ask him some questions."

Another lie. Ed saw it as clearly as if a neon sign had lit up over her head. Was this Gaia, the person who had been his closest friend for the last four months? Was this the same girl he longed for with an almost frightening intensity?

Yes. It was.

"That's not true," Ed said evenly, looking into Gaia's eyes. "You're looking for Skizz, and it isn't to ask him some questions."

"Well, don't worry about it," Gaia said. She looked around with studied casualness. She shifted her feet. Obviously she wanted him gone.

Ed suddenly felt afraid. Afraid for Gaia, afraid *of* Gaia.

"Look, let's go get a cup of coffee," he said. "Let's get out of here."

Gaia looked at the ground, scuffing her boots against the cobblestones.

"Gaia, come on," Ed said. "You don't want to be here."

"You don't know anything about what I want."

When he looked into her face, he didn't recognize her. "Please, Gaia. Come on. Don't do this." Whatever "this" was.

"Just leave me alone!" she snapped, and she whirled and disappeared into the darkness without a sound.

A cold feeling of dread settled over Ed's heart as he stared blankly at the spot where she had stood moments before.

Last night I did the strangest thing. It was after Ed found me in Washington Square Park. I was freaking and didn't know what to do. So I headed up St. Mark's Place and ducked into a thrift shop for a few minutes, trying to get my act together. Then I looked out the plate glass window, and right across the street was this old, crumbly, odd-looking church.

I crossed the street and read its sign. It was a Russian Orthodox church. Is that bizarre or what? Only in New York.

Anyway, I went up the steps and tried one of the heavy wooden doors. There was graffiti sprayed onto the front of the building. Gang signs. But the door opened. Inside, it was cool and dim and smelled heavily of incense. I haven't been inside many churches in my life, but here I was, just a few minutes after I had been in the park planning to murder

someone. I felt like I was in an
episode of *The X-Files* .

There were people up by the
altar, polishing brass candle-
sticks, and someone running a
vacuum on the worn red carpet.
There were no pews, so I leaned
against a cool stone column for a
while. It was strange, being
inside that church, so late at
night. So quiet, so peaceful. So
different from the things going
on inside my head.

Don't get me wrong, I'm not
much of a believer. But right
then and there, for some reason,
I said a prayer for forgiveness.

he was still
shocked when
the first
thin threads
of pain
registered
in his
brain . . .

kind

of

an

asshole

NOTE TO MYSELF: SCRATCH BEING AN undercover agent as a possible career. Not only is a guy in a wheelchair kind of hard to disguise, but he's also so freaking slow!

Ed's Going Down

Ed paused at the corner of Broadway and Waverly Place, his hot go-cup of latte perched in the screw-on armrest cup holder his aunt had given him for Christmas. Where had she gotten it? he wondered. Wheelchairs R Us? He had to admit it came in handy.

When the light turned green, Ed spun his wheels, moving aggressively through the crowd. He knew people usually didn't mind being bumped by a cripple in a chair. They would turn around, ready to glare, ready to curse him out, then catch sight of him. Seeing a young man in a wheelchair usually calmed them right down.

Gaia had managed to completely give him the slip again after school. They had eaten lunch together like two chewing statues. She hadn't even bothered making an excuse as to why she'd split on him last night or why they couldn't get together tonight, a Friday night.

Now, as Ed bumped up the handicapped-accessible sidewalk ramp, he remembered how tired Gaia had looked. Her nose had been running, and she'd wiped it on her sleeve. He knew without a doubt that she had been out late, in the cold, hunting Skizz, but somehow the crowded cafeteria of the Village School hadn't seemed like the best place to confront her.

Ed was pretty much at the end of his rope with Gaia. It had been five long days since Mary's death, and Gaia had hardly said more than three sentences to him. Then last night had been so weird. What was she thinking? What was she planning? He had to know. Which was why he had already checked the Starbucks on Astor Place and made a complete circuit of Washington Square Park. No Gaia. His arms and shoulders were going to look like Hulk Hogan's if he kept getting these kinds of workouts.

Now he was going to hit Tompkins Square Park. The whole idea of Gaia lying in wait for Skizz made his blood run cold. She'd already beaten the crap out of Skizz once. What else could she do?

Ed was tired. He was three blocks from the park. He took a sip of his coffee, enjoying the way the warmth seeped down through his esophagus and pooled in his stomach.

"Hey!" he cried angrily as a hand sharply knocked his coffee away. Instinctively he grabbed his wheels, only to be stopped by a long, wavy knife blade shoved under his nose. He could feel the sharp edge, cold against his skin.

"Don't move."

Oh, shit.

His attacker wasn't that big, just a young street kid of indeterminate age and race, his hair wrapped up in a bandanna. There was a small, homemade-looking tattoo of a sun right in the middle of his forehead. His upper lip had `dark, downy fuzz`, and small, unevenly mowed tufts of stubble blotched his chin.

"Gimme your money." The command was quiet but had an underlying thread of desperation.

Without warning, Ed was flooded with an adrenaline-soaked rage. He knew that before his accident, he would have been five inches taller than this jerk and outweighed him by forty pounds. This guy never would have picked him as a mark. But here he was, `Mr. Victim in a Wheelchair`. His stomach roiled, and a bitter taste rose in the back of his throat. This sucked.

"Give it!" the mugger said, and quickly flicked his knifepoint across Ed's cheek.

Since knowing Gaia, Ed had been witness to more acts of violence than he had in his whole previous Gaia-less existence. And yet he was still shocked when the first thin threads of pain registered in his brain and still scared by the unnaturally hot flow of blood down his cheek.

Hating himself, hating the way his hand was shaking, Ed reached into the inner pocket of his jacket and pulled out his wallet. He remembered with grim, futile satisfaction that he had just spent his last five dollars at Starbucks, and only that morning his mom had asked for her Visa card back because she was getting a new one.

But the mugger wasn't going to check it out here. He took the wallet, sheathed the knife, and spun. He was gone, out of sight, before Ed could count to seven.

Well, shit. His heart was pounding loud in his ears; his hands were trembling. He reached up to touch his burning cheek and saw his leather glove shiny and dark with blood. A thought hit him like a hammer: Ed was desperate for Gaia's presence. If she had been here, this never would have happened. She would have kicked that guy's ass from here till Tuesday. Ed would have been avenged.

The realization was like being punched in the chest, and for a moment Ed literally couldn't breathe. A short time ago he'd been tall for his age, starting to get his adult weight, his grown-man muscle. He'd been the biggest, baddest daredevil on a board this side of America. Now what was he?

When he reached First Avenue, he turned for home. Forget the park right now. Forget Gaia. People glanced at him in alarm, then quickly turned away. He probably looked like some whacked-out Desert Storm vet, rolling along with a murderous expression and a bloody cheek. He ignored them. He'd learned how to ignore a lot of stares in the last couple of years.

At his apartment building Ed wheeled through the automatic doors. He crossed the lobby and rolled inside the elevator, pushing hard to get over the little gap in the floor. Automatically he punched his button. His cheek felt thick and sticky. There was a knot in his throat he couldn't swallow.

Once Ed had been tough, strong. When he and Heather were together, she had relied on *him*. And other guys had steered clear of his territory. He was cool. He was Shred. He had probably been kind of an asshole, if you wanted to know the truth. But at least he hadn't been pathetic.

Dinner with the Gannises

"PLEASE PASS THE SALT STUFF," Mr. Gannis said, motioning to the middle of the table.

"The substitute?" Heather's mother asked.

"Yes," said Mr. Gannis.

Heather sat quietly, cutting her chicken breast into little squares, scooping up bits of scalloped potatoes. Since her father's heart attack two years ago, he'd been on a low-salt diet. Her mother couldn't eat shellfish. Now Phoebe was practically starving herself. Did everyone in her family have bizarro eating issues except her?

Heather glanced across the table at her other sister, Lauren. Lauren was twenty and finishing her undergrad degree at Parsons. She was shoveling in her dinner with enthusiasm. A few days ago Heather would have been disgusted by her sister's huge appetite. Now she was grateful that at least one family member appeared to have *some* sanity.

Why didn't anyone seem to notice that Phoebe had eaten only half a salad so far, with no dressing? That she was just pushing the chicken around on her plate? Now that Heather was hyperaware of Phoebe's eating habits, it stunned her that she hadn't noticed them before. It left her feeling helpless and angry.

Who could she talk to about this? Sam? Maybe— except the next time she saw him, she wanted him to focus on her, not Phoebe. Her mother? No, her mom believed that you could never be too rich or too thin. Her father would simply refer Heather to her mother. Lauren would be no help at all. What about Heather's friends? Instinctively Heather shrank from the thought of confiding in any of them. She still hadn't let on to anyone about her family's finances, or lack thereof, and she knew that Phoebe's eating disorder would simply become a hot gossip topic. It wasn't any of their business.

What Heather needed was a *real* friend. Just one good friend.

You know, Mary, when you were
alive, I was starting to feel
like I was sort of almost normal.
I mean, I had friends (you and
Ed), I was going to school, I was
in love with someone (Sam), I was
doing normal teenagery things.
Now you're gone, and I'm like the
poster girl for dysfunction. I
can't deal with school. I can't
deal with Ed. I saw Sam yesterday, and it was awful. Everything
out of my mouth was the opposite
of what I wanted to say.

Why is my life such an unend-
ing horror show? What do I have
to do to make it bearable?

I am tottering on the brink.
I'm almost afraid of *myself*.

I've seen the look in her eyes. I know that look because I've seen it too many times to name. I've seen it in the heartless gazes of trained assassins. Sometimes I've seen it when I've looked in the mirror. I know all too well what it means.

Gaia is after her friend's murderer. She wants to kill him. She wants to make him pay for what he did. Understandable under the circumstances. Who wouldn't fantasize about doing the same if someone they loved were brutally murdered?

Believe me, Gaia, I understand.

But Gaia can't afford to do as others do. She can't afford to have fantasies of revenge. Because unlike most people, Gaia is capable of following those fantasies through.

And once she does, once she has a taste for blood, I don't know if she can ever go back. Not someone like her—born to fight,

TOM MOORE

physically and mentally built to
destroy anything that gets in her
way. Built to kill.

I'm watching you, Gaia. I'm
waiting for you to make your
move. But I can't protect you
from yourself. You've got to do
that.

I believe in you.

Do you believe in me?

Then without a
conscious
thought she
was
moving, **daddy's**
sprinting **little**
down the
cobbled walk **girl**
with her hair
flying in back
of her . . .

IT'S A UNIVERSAL LAW THAT IF

you drop anything on the floor within a ten-foot radius of a bed, that object will slowly and surely be sucked underneath the bed by some unseen magnetic force.

Red and Green M&M's

Or at least that's the theory Gaia came up with on Saturday morning when she was searching desperately for her only working pen. It had mysteriously disappeared when she took a bathroom break. Now she was on her hands and knees, swatting aside dust bunnies and pushing aside her ancient, faded quilt.

Eureka. There it was. With a large sweeping gesture Gaia fished the pen out from under her bed, her arm coming out covered with large clumps of dust and quite a few long blond hairs.

A thin, stiff piece of paper was stuck to her sleeve, and Gaia pulled it off, then froze. It was a note. Little red and green stains had smudged some of the words, but Gaia knew instantly what the note said.

Sinking back on her haunches, Gaia read the apology letter she held in her hand, a fresh wave of pain washing over her. It was from Mary. From when Mary had kicked coke and asked Gaia to be her friend again.

Gaia rubbed her finger along the page, stained with the colors of the M&M's Mary had included with the note. How could these words still be here when Mary was gone? She continued to feel the texture where the pen had scratched the paper. Maybe by touching the grooves, the indents, she could touch the person who had left them there. If only . . .

"Gaia! Telephone!" Ella's strident voice ripped through Gaia's thoughts like a knife. Gaia winced and stood up, almost tripping on a moldering pile of laundry. She scooped it up in one arm and went downstairs, trying to make her mind blank. She needed to have her guard up to deal with Ella.

Still holding the laundry, Gaia entered the first-floor kitchen and wordlessly took the phone from Ella. Her foster mother's fingernails were long and blood-red, as though she had just plucked out the heart of a victim and hadn't rinsed off yet.

Gaia cradled the phone between her shoulder and ear, trying not to drop her laundry.

"Hello?" she said, already knowing it was Ed. No one else ever called her. Not Sam. Certainly not her father, wherever the hell he was.

"Gaia?" said a woman's husky, unfamiliar voice.

Gaia's neck prickled. Alarm bells went off. "Yes?" she said tightly.

"This is Patricia Moss. Mary's mother."

Oh, crap. Double crap.

"How are you, dear?"

"Um . . ."

"I know. We all feel that way," said Mrs. Moss. "I've been worried about you. Did Mr. Niven tell you I phoned?"

Yep. She had found his note, taped to her bedroom door.

"Yes, he did," Gaia said.

"Well, do come see us, dear, if you feel up to it," Mrs. Moss went on quietly. "Now, I wanted to tell you—Mary's . . . funeral is next Wednesday, at eleven o'clock, at the Riverside Chapel. We were thinking . . . it would mean a lot to us—to all of us—if you would agree to speak."

"What?" Gaia's voice sounded like it had been planed down to a thin rasp.

"If you would say a few words at Mary's funeral," continued Mrs. Moss. "I know you weren't friends for very long, but we feel that in some ways, you were her only true friend."

Why? Because I got her killed? Because I went too far with her drug dealer, and he paid someone to shoot your daughter in retaliation? Gaia felt something like hysteria rising in her throat.

"Because you were the one who made her face— made all of us face—her problems," said Mrs. Moss. "Please—it would mean a lot to us."

This was too horrible, too awful to contemplate. "I'm sorry, I can't," Gaia said curtly. She hung up the phone before Mrs. Moss could say any more, then whirled to see Ella, leaning against the wall, smoking a cigarette. Was that the hint of a smile? Gaia suddenly had the sensation that Ella was a cat and that she, Gaia, was a slab of tuna.

"Dear, dear," Ella crooned in honeyed tones. "Was that poor Mrs. Moss? That poor woman. To lose your daughter that way . . ."

Gaia frowned. To have Ella even mention Mary's name was more repulsive than she could stomach. She remembered when Ella had finally goaded Gaia into punching her, about a month ago. If Ella didn't watch it, they were going there again.

"What do you know about it?" Gaia said coldly. She knew she hadn't mentioned Mary's death to the Nivens.

Ella produced a newspaper from behind her back. "Only what I read," she answered smoothly. "What a shame. That innocent girl—they say it looked like a drug hit. No doubt some awful dealer got her hooked. Maybe she owed him money or something."

Gaia felt her blood starting to pound in her ears.

"And they didn't even catch him," Ella went on. "That monster is still out there, preying on other innocent girls."

Her words spiked into Gaia's chest as if they were

barbecue skewers. A dull pain roared in Gaia's head. Today. Gaia had to find Skizz today. Blindly she stumbled over to the laundry room and threw her clothes into the washing machine. She measured out a cup of detergent and closed the lid. If only she could rid the world of Ella *and* Skizz in one fell swoop. The machine started to chug, and Gaia leaned against it, her knuckles white as they gripped the sides.

Okay, calm down. You have a plan. Ironically, her father's words came back to her. *Don't let emotion— not anger, not pain, not love—cloud your actions. That will get you killed.*

Gaia paused. Scratch that last bit. She wasn't daddy's little girl anymore. She didn't need his advice.

Screw him.

"UM, GAIA?" GEORGE SAID, TAPPING on her open door.

"Yeah?" Gaia looked up from her bed, where she was putting on socks still warm from the dryer. Ecstasy.

"Ella and I thought it would be nice to take a drive out into

Get Some Fresh Air

the country. You know, get out of the city, get some fresh air. Maybe stop at a little restaurant and have dinner. We'd like for you to come with us."

It was actually tempting. Gaia longed to be somewhere out of the city, somewhere where snow was really snow. But two things held her back: Gaia was about to head out to hunt for Skizz, and there was no way she would be cooped up in a car with Ella for more than, say, ten seconds.

Gaia sighed regretfully. "I'm sorry, George. It does sound kind of . . . *neat*, but I better get to the library and work on my paper."

George shrugged. "Oh, well, maybe some other time. Don't work too hard, now. Will you be okay for dinner? We might not get back till late."

"I'll be fine," Gaia said. "You guys have fun." After George left, Gaia shook her head and took a deep breath. George was another person who would be horrified and disappointed in her if he knew her plans for Skizz. For an instant she pictured herself in prison, in handcuffs, looking out through a cell's bars at Ed and George. And Mary. Shivering, Gaia blinked and erased the image from her mind.

Twenty minutes later, after she was sure George and Cruella had left, Gaia put on her leaking down jacket and headed downstairs, leaving bits of ragged feathers every third step. Her stomach was tight, and she felt unbearably tense. Was this really her, planning to murder someone?

Yes. It was. She was going to do it.

Just as Gaia was reaching for the front door, a thought hit her: gloves. Her hands were already dry and chapped. Maybe the Nivens had some spares.

In the hall closet Gaia found a pair of white mohair gloves edged with fake leopard skin. So practical. Gaia pushed behind the coats to the wall shelves. Bingo. Next to a small red box shoved into the corner was a pair of George's leather gloves, lined with Thinsulate. Ah. They were only a tiny bit too big, thanks to her `huge, gorillalike paws`. Perfect. She arranged the other gloves neatly on the shelf, then backed out of the closet.

As she was about to close the door, the red box caught her attention. Shiny wrapping paper. It looked like it could be a leftover Christmas present, but that didn't compute. Ella wasn't the kind of woman to leave any kind of present unopened for very long.

Gaia picked up the box, shook it a few times. She could hear all the pieces jiggling around inside. Curiosity almost prompted her to open it. Almost.

She shrugged and stuffed the box back up on the shelf. It was probably some cheap costume jewelry from one of Ella's secret admirers. `How lame.` The idea made Gaia's stomach turn. Or had it been turning already?

Outside, the sun was just setting. The air was cold,

but not as damp as it had been. Maybe no more snow tonight. Almost instantly, as Gaia headed down Perry Street, her nose started running. This time she was prepared, though, and she pulled a wad of toilet paper from her pocket and mopped up the worst of it.

If she walked fast, she could make Washington Square Park in fifteen minutes. If she stopped for a chickpea roti at one of the many little delis on the way, she could add two minutes to that time. Her stomach felt kind of upset, but maybe she should eat, anyway. Low blood sugar would make her feel shakier than she already did. Today was the day. She could feel it.

It was weird about Skizz. The last time Gaia had seen him, he had looked like something the dog had brought in. Gaia had definitely gone overboard. The truth was, she had practically beaten him to death. Now, not even two weeks later, he should still be in pretty bad shape. And he *had* been in bad shape when Gaia had last seen him. He'd been a mess. But apparently not too much of a mess to hire some sleazeball to do his dirty work for him.

Gaia strode along, walking fast to keep warm, licking spicy curried chickpeas off her gloves.

The West Fourth Street entrance to the park was right on the corner, and Gaia headed in. It was dark in this corner, the overhead lamps burned out. Hands by her sides, she moved forward toward the center of the park. First a quick check by the chess tables, out of habit, then a circuit around the park perimeter.

"Smoke, smoke, smoke," offered a tall, thin guy in a rasta hat.

"No, thanks," Gaia said, and kept moving.

At the chess tables Zolov sat before an empty seat. Gaia wished she had twenty minutes and twenty bucks. A couple of other regulars were packing up their pieces, getting ready to head in out of the cold and dark. On a January night the only people still offering a game were players who were so chess obsessed they didn't feel the cold or so desperate they didn't have anyplace else to go.

Of course, Sam wasn't there. He was probably safe and warm in his dorm room. Probably with Heather. She was probably rubbing his shoulders.

Oh, stop it!

No sign of Skizz so far. Was he lying low after the murder? It seemed uncharacteristically sensible of him.

Not that the park was devoid of weirdos and various lowlifes. She'd barely made one circuit of the perimeter and had already been approached about eight times. Why was it that pond scum guys always seemed to think they had a chance just because she was alone, just because she was female? A while ago Gaia would have been happy to provide a graphic demonstration of just how wrong they were. Tonight she didn't have time.

As Gaia was heading out the park's Waverly Street entrance, planning to circle the block, she caught a glimpse of a figure about sixty yards ahead. It was night, but the guy moved under a lamppost. . . . His dark, shapeless coat was bulky, a black knitted cap pulled low on his Neanderthal brow. One arm was in a sling. The other hand—yes. It was taped.

Skizz.

Gaia froze less than a second. Then without a conscious thought she was moving, sprinting down the cobbled walk with her hair flying in back of her, the wind streaming icily over her taut face.

She was going to do it. She wasn't sure how, but she was sure of the outcome. She was going to kill Skizz.

Raw power pumped through her veins. Her arms were already coiled, iron hard, ready to crush his skull. Her eyes lasered in on him, pinning him to one spot as she flashed forward. *Time to die.*

Gaia sensed the car before she actually saw it.

A dark, beat-up sedan screeched to a halt by Skizz, the back door already popped open.

No.

No, no, no. There was no way.

As Skizz moved toward the car, Gaia poured on the power. She was almost to him. Thirty more feet, twenty. Her boots sounded like muffled thunder on the sidewalk. She just needed to . . .

Skizz stepped into the sedan, slamming the door behind him. The car lurched into traffic, moving away from her.

Oh God! No! Get back here, you son of a bitch! You killed Mary! I have to do this now! For a moment Gaia was desolate, panting and gasping for breath. Then grim purpose hardened her face, and she raced into the street. She could catch that car. She could do it. She was faster than anyone. She would catch the car, yank open the door, and rip Skizz from its interior. With any luck his legs would be crushed beneath the car wheels.

Gaia raced after the dark car, the hard street shocking her joints as she ran. Her fury made her feel like an arrow, streaking through the cold air. When she caught the car, she would jump onto the trunk and hang on. Then when it stopped, she could—

The next thing Gaia knew, she was taking a dive into the curb. Several things registered all at once: screeching brakes, honking horns, traffic lights flashing crazily above her, and another person tumbling down on top of her.

Moaning, Gaia tried to curl into a ball, her shaky hands struggling to push her way out from under this other human being.

"Are you crazy?" a voice demanded roughly. "Were you trying to kill yourself? You ran right into me!"

A man's face, concerned and angry and scared, floated over her as he stood up shakily.

"Unh," Gaia managed, gasping for breath. Her heart still pounded. She knew Skizz was gone. If she were the kind of girl who cried, she would have wept with frustration and rage. She'd been stalking him for days, and this was the first sighting she'd had. Now he was gone. Dammit!

"Look, I'm calling an ambulance," said the guy. He pulled a cell phone out of his suit pocket and started to punch in numbers. "You look pretty scratched up." He glanced down at his own, unharmed body, then at Gaia. "I guess you broke my fall. What the hell were you running for, anyway?" People kept walking by as Gaia gingerly rubbed the side of her leg that had hit the curb hardest. At that moment she was glad of the typical New Yorker's aversion to getting involved.

"I'm all right," Gaia managed. She tried to sit up, but a fresh wave of pain made her sag. "Don't call an ambulance."

The man hesitated. "I better," he decided. "Something could be broken. You were going pretty fast."

Shaking her head, Gaia said, "No. Nothing's broken." She wiggled her foot to show him, even though it hurt so much, she sucked in air with a whoosh. "I'm fine," she choked out.

"Can you stand?"

"Uh-huh," she said, not knowing if she could or not. Knowing she had to. The guy gave her his hand, and Gaia, gritting her teeth at both the pain and the fact that she had to allow a stranger to help her, raggedly rose to her feet. As long as she didn't put weight on her right side, she was fine. God, how fast had she been running to hit the curb that hard? Sweat beaded on her forehead. She felt dizzy and sick. Her hip really, really hurt.

"Where do you live?" asked the guy.

"Perry Street. Not far." What did it matter if he knew? What did it matter? So what if he were a random psycho in a chalk-stripe suit? So what if he was about to kidnap her and kill her? No big deal. Gaia tried to control her breathing, started the mental exercises that would allow her to negate the pain. She touched her right foot to the sidewalk. Her leg didn't buckle, though a bolt of white-hot pain shot up her leg and almost made her moan. Nothing was broken.

"Why don't I flag you a cab?" The man seemed uncertain, as if she might sue him for walking in the wrong place at the wrong time. The whole experience of living with New York paranoia suddenly struck Gaia as ridiculous, horrible, and funny. It would also have been a little bit scary if Gaia could feel fear.

Gaia nodded. "Maybe that would be best."

Back at the brownstone, she opened the door, then locked it behind her without looking back. Her forehead felt cold and clammy with sweat. Leaning against the wall, she limped slowly down the hallway to the little powder room tucked under the stairs. Silently Gaia gave thanks that George and Cruella were still out. Then she opened the toilet lid, leaned over, and barfed.

Okay, I've decided to give
Gaia a call. I know, I know. I'm
a glutton for punishment. After
the way she's treated me—okay—
stomped all over my heart, I
should just let her stay on her
polar ice cap and blow her off
forever. That's what she said she
wants.

But I've been thinking, and
there have been times in the last
four months when I felt like I
caught a glimpse of the Gaia
beneath the mask. Just a glimpse,
when she let her guard slip, let
her real self shine through. When
that happened, I saw not a super-
woman, not a Norse goddess, but
just a girl. Just a girl with no
parents and no other friends but
me. And maybe that girl needs my
help. Even if she doesn't realize
it yet.

Gaia wanted
to go below **a**
permanent
twilight
the
belt? Fine.

"HOW BADLY IS SHE HURT?" LOKI

Limited Usefulness

subdued the acidic thread of anger in his voice as he buttoned up his shirt. Ella was still sitting on the bed, one foot dangling lazily over the edge. Loki's hands clenched and unclenched by his sides. He turned toward the window, furious that Ella hadn't told him of this development as soon as she had arrived at his apartment.

In the reflection of the window he saw Ella shrug.

He waited.

"Nothing's broken," Ella said finally. "She must have a bad bruise, but I haven't seen it. Unless you want to add peeping at her in her bath to my list of duties."

Loki's stomach tightened. This foolish, shortsighted woman. If she had two brain cells left to rub together, she would be anxiously *trying* to add duties to her list. Obviously she had no idea of her increasingly limited usefulness to him. In and *out* of bed. Had she not thought ahead as to what her future would be when she could no longer serve him? Did she assume he would simply wave good-bye and let her go live somewhere happily ever after? Did she assume Loki would trust her to keep all his secrets? Did she assume he would keep her on as his lover?

Smoothly he turned to her. Soon it would be time for her distressingly inadequate service to end. In the meantime she did provide a conduit of information that would be hard to duplicate.

"No," he said evenly. "But you might keep an eye on her. If she needs medical attention, see to it."

"She won't need medical attention," Ella said, fishing out a cigarette and tapping it against her wrist. She started to light it but was stopped by Loki's glacial gaze. "She's indestructible." She sounded bitter about it. Loki suppressed a smile.

"Luckily for you," he said, keeping his voice hard.

"I can't keep her locked in her room," Ella protested.

"No. But you can do your job," Loki said. "Do try, will you?"

"Yes," Ella said.

"You are dismissed." Loki turned away again.

After Ella had resentfully slunk out of the apartment, Loki permitted himself the pleasure of ruminating on Gaia. It was almost time. Despite his anger at Ella for not eliminating the dealer yet, still, Loki was pleased. According to his report, Gaia had been absolutely hell-bent on the kill. Would she do it? Would she cross the line? It was a tantalizing notion. If she did, he could finally make his move.

"GAIA? HEY."

Hesitation. "Hey." She sounded distant. Like that was new. Ed shifted in his bed, switching the phone to his other ear and punching his pillow a couple of times. His thin legs barely made ridges beneath his down comforter.

Worth Shot

"Listen, I'm going to give you another chance." Silence at the other end. "How are you doing?"

"I'm doing fine," Gaia replied, already sounding testy.

"Well, can we get together? I have a whole list of new complaints about my parents and no one to listen to me."

Silence while he imagined Gaia smiling.

"Ed, listen," she said haltingly.

Ed the basset hound pricked up his ears. Was she giving in? He couldn't wait for her to see his face, with its knife cut going across his cheek. Then she would be sorry. Then she would be all concerned about him, full of anger at his mugging. It would be great.

"I'm not interested. Okay?" Gaia continued.

Ouch. Ed almost slammed down the receiver, but some perverse impulse made him pull it back to his ear. Gaia wanted to go below the belt? Fine.

"Interested in what, Gaia? Looking for Skizz? Or

have you found him yet? I didn't read about any bodies being found in the East River. Or maybe you were planning to dispose of him in the Hudson. I'm out of the loop with what all the young murderers are doing with their prey these days."

"Very amusing," Gaia said, her voice sounding muffled. Her tone had dropped from chilly to below freezing.

Now what? He'd blown this sky-high one minute into the conversation.

"Gaia, just talk to me," he said.

He was such a pathetic sucker.

"Ed, I don't want to talk."

No shit. Ed's jaw set as he tried to keep himself from blurting out, "I got mugged!" He wouldn't stoop that low. He wouldn't use his near-death experience to get Gaia to show some sympathy and interest.

Ed willed a snappy comeback to pop into his mind. He'd already used "whatever" the last time he'd hung up on her. Maybe he should come up with a list and keep it by the phone. How to hang up on Gaia: fifty different ways. He was sure it would come in handy.

After racking his brain for a cool, disinterested, sarcastic line for a full twelve seconds, Ed found himself saying the one thing he hadn't planned on.

"You're going to realize you need me," he said in a low, harsh voice. "When you do, you'll be lucky if I'm still here."

There. That was it. The perfect last word. What could she possibly say to that?

"Ed. I don't need you. I don't want you. I'm sorry but I don't see how you—a neurotic guy in a wheel-chair—could actually help *me*."

Ed was too stunned to breathe.

"It's not that I don't want to talk now, or tomorrow, or next week, or whatever. I don't want to talk ever. I don't want you in my life," Gaia hissed. Ed swallowed. "Get the hell out of my life."

The phone went dead. Before he could really comprehend what had just happened, Ed felt the tears coursing down his cheeks.

"ED?" MRS. FARGO CALLED FROM outside the door.

Ed was still clutching the cordless phone as he lay back against three huge, puffy pillows. From his bed he could see the hazy

Later

January sky trying to convince him it was truly daytime and not a permanent bleak twilight.

"Yeah?"

The door opened, and his mother came in, dressed for success in camel flannel slacks, a matching cashmere twinset, and a discreet pearl choker at her throat. Ed was sure his sister's fiancé's parents would be suitably impressed. Today the two sets of parents were meeting at the Russian Tea Room to discuss wedding plans. Ed hadn't been invited, thank God.

"Honey, it's almost eleven o'clock," his mother said. "Shouldn't you get up and get dressed?"

This was obviously a rhetorical question.

"Yeah, okay," said Ed.

"Have you done your exercises?" Mrs. Fargo asked, automatically picking up clothes and folding them over the back of a chair.

"Not yet."

His mother's eyes met his, and Ed waited. She was obviously warring with herself, trying to determine how much to nag him. Ed breathed a sigh of relief when he saw she'd decided against it for today.

"Your father and I will probably be gone until about three. There's food in the kitchen. Do you need anything?" She paused in the doorway.

"No, I'm fine," said Ed.

"Okay, then. See you later." The door shut silently.

As Ed began to do the repetitive stretching movements that kept his leg muscles from atrophying further, he realized that his mother was making progress. For almost six months after the accident she had refused to leave him alone in the house in case he fell or needed something. In case he would commit suicide while they were out.

For her to leave with such a show of casualness was a big step forward. Ed grunted as he gripped his left ankle and flexed it. It didn't hurt, of course, but he could feel his back muscles pulling. Forty minutes of this, then half an hour of free weights for upper-body strength. Months ago, when Ed had decided that he would go on living even in this form, he had realized there were things he could do that would marginally improve his existence. Trying to keep what was left of his body in shape was one of them. Making friends, keeping connected to other people, was another. Trying to date, to think of himself and others in a romantic, sexual way, was a third.

It seemed like he was down to one out of three. He knew he needed somebody—a friend, a lover. He had been hoping Gaia was that person. But maybe he needed to reexamine his options.

"LOOK AT THIS PILE OF CRAP,"

Heather said in disgust. Phoebe glanced up from her magazine, looked around the room, and nodded. Piles of clothes were on every spare surface of Heather's bedroom. They almost swamped Phoebe on the bed and covered

Making Sam Hee

the small rocker in the corner and most of the floor.

"This is a humongous pile of crap," Heather said again. "All this stuff and I can't find one cute outfit."

"I know what you mean," said Phoebe. "All of my stuff is horrible—totally last year. And it doesn't fit. I just want to go shopping all day long and get some stuff that's decent."

Heather sagged against her bed. "Me too."

In the past day or two Heather had been trying to think of what to do about Phoebe's condition. She couldn't tell her friends, and she hadn't seen Sam in days. Who else was there? She just had to shut up about it and try to enjoy hanging out with Phoebe without talking about anything controversial. Like food. Or weight. Or bodies.

Before all this happened, Heather wouldn't have believed how often and in how many different situations a person could mention one of those topics. Staying off these subjects reduced her conversation by about eighty percent. She thought about all the times she had moaned about her weight or her size or her waistline. Now she wished she hadn't wasted her breath.

"Feeb—what's going to happen?" Heather asked.

Phoebe looked up, her face closing.

"I mean about Dad, and the money and all," Heather clarified. "I mean, how long am I supposed to wear these clothes?" Of course, the question was bigger than that, and both sisters knew it.

Taking a deep breath, Phoebe said, "I don't know. Mom said something once about Grandma Nancy helping out, but I don't know what that means."

"Do you think Mom is going back to work?" Heather asked.

"Get real," Phoebe scoffed. "What would all her friends think? No, I think Mom and Dad are just going to keep doing what they're doing and hope it all turns out okay."

"But—"

"Listen, try not to worry about it," Phoebe advised, rolling off Heather's bed and standing up. In her black leggings and wide-wale corduroy shirt she looked model thin and chic. Except that her leggings were baggy. Heather didn't know Lycra could *be* baggy. "Everything will be okay. I've got to get over to Sasha's house. See you later."

"Later," said Heather.

For three minutes Heather lay among the pile of clothes on her bed, wallowing in self-pity. Then she remembered that she was Heather Gannis, dammit, and she deserved better than this. Even from herself.

She picked up the phone and hit memory dial #1. Sam himself actually answered. Miracle of miracles.

"Hi, Sam. It's me," Heather said, feeling the warm fuzzies starting to come over her.

"Hi," Sam replied. His voice was so adorable,

so husky, sexy. "I feel like it's been ages since I saw you. We really need to get together."

"Yeah, we do," Heather agreed happily. "I really miss you. How's the studying going?"

Sam groaned. "I feel like I live at the library. I only came home to shower."

"But the semester just started," Heather felt compelled to point out.

"I know. I'm just trying to get off on the right foot. I've got four bitch classes this semester, and I've got to finish that incomplete in comparative anatomy from last semester."

The warm fuzzies were being slowly, surely replaced by a feeling of resentment. "Sam," Heather began, trying to keep her voice reasonable. "We're supposed to be going out. Supposed to be boyfriend and girlfriend. But we never see each other anymore. I mean, I spent New Year's with my *girlfriends!*"

A sigh on the other end.

"You're right," came Sam's unbelievable answer.

Hope bloomed once more.

"I'm sorry," he continued. "Dad gave me such a hard time over Christmas that I kind of freaked out about my grades. But you're right—I can't study twenty-four hours a day. And we *do* need to talk."

"Not just talk," Heather said suggestively. She was smiling and twirling the phone cord around her wrist. Finally Sam was saying some things she actually felt like hearing. There was a chance he just might come through for her after all. She could even tell him about Phoebe. After all, he was premed. He might have some idea what Heather could do.

"Yeah. Listen, what about tomorrow?" Sam suggested. "After classes I'll take the day off from studying. Unless . . . are you busy after school?"

"Nope," Heather said happily. "I could come over to your place. We could hang out for a while, maybe get something to eat over on MacDougal. I just want to see you."

"Yeah, okay," Sam said. "See you tomorrow."

"Bye, Sam," Heather said. "Can't wait to see you."

He'd already hung up.

They might
play this
game out for
another
hour, but
the end
was
now certain.
Gaia would
win.

never

show

weakness

TRY AS HE MIGHT, ED COULDN'T

No Matter How Cold

think of a single thing worse than a freezing, wet Monday morning in January when he had to go to school, when Gaia had completely ripped out his heart and was probably doing reckless, dangerous, or stupid things or all three, when he had just lost one of his good friends, and when he had a very visible cut on his cheek from getting mugged over the weekend. Was there anything that could be worse? He thought about it for a second.

Ed's locker was on the lower tier, of course, since he'd lost almost three feet in height since junior year. Wheeling up to it, he flipped open its combination lock and started to rummage through the unorganized mess inside, looking for something resembling this morning's books.

Okay, here's a thought: Ed wakes up; there's nothing for breakfast except Fiber One cereal. Over breakfast his folks tell him they're getting divorced because his dad has decided he was meant to be a woman and is having a sex change. Right after that announcement their house catches on fire and burns to the ground, and Ed is carried out of the burning building in nothing but his boxers. Outside in the freezing weather in his boxers, with his scrawny white legs showing, every hot girl he's ever wanted shows up and sees him. Well, okay, that might be worse than the way he felt this morning.

Clawing through the wreckage in his locker, Ed pulled out some notebooks and a couple of possibly appropriate textbooks and dropped them into one of the side bags attached to his wheelchair. Side bags, cup holders—what was next? Maybe some kind of James Bond rocket engines strapped to the back so Ed could shoot down school corridors at Mach 1.

Ed laughed hollowly at this scenario as the school bell rang and the halls suddenly emptied. Like rats, students scurried into classes, books tucked under their arms. Ed slammed his locker shut and started to wheel off to his first class. Then he saw a tall, slim, wild-haired goddess stride around the corner and fling open her locker. As usual, Gaia had avoided being on time. Her mouth pressed into a thin line, she stooped to drop her bag on the ground, then straightened slowly to rifle through her locker contents. Ed saw her find a forgotten, half-smushed Ding Dongs package, which she tucked into her bag with satisfaction.

Every time he saw Gaia, Ed's heart sped up, his breathing quickened, his pupils dilated. For some reason—okay, a million reasons—Gaia was very special to him. But today things were going to be different. She had stepped over the line. He knew she hadn't meant what she said. Couldn't have meant it. But that didn't make it any less hurtful.

Slowly Ed rolled down the hall. He had to pass her to get to his first class, just as she had to pass him to get to her chem lab. In an instant a dozen different scenarios raced through his head as he considered his approach. How should he be? Reproachful, normal, angry, mean, sad? He decided to just ignore her.

As usual, Gaia took the initiative away from him. As he was formulating the perfect greeting, she looked up, glanced at his face, and frowned.

"What happened to you? Cut yourself shaving?"

For one awful second Ed had a flashback to Friday night, being mugged in the dark by some scumbag with a knife. He could have been killed. As it was, his wallet and his pride had been ripped away from him, leaving him wanting to crawl into a dark hole and disappear. And this is the concern he got? A frown and a snappy remark? Besides, he thought Gaia didn't want to talk to him. Wasn't that what she had said?

Suddenly Ed was very tired. Tired of not getting what he needed from someone he'd thought was his best friend. Tired of playing games to get Gaia to notice him, to take him seriously, to feel for him what he felt for her. He was exhausted—too exhausted to play anymore.

"Mugged by asshole with knife," Ed said shortly, continuing on past Gaia.

A strong hand reached out and yanked his wheelchair to a halt. Blue eyes bored into his, then flicked across his cut cheek, assessing the damage. In that moment Ed saw concern, anger, sympathy, and some unnamable emotion in Gaia's eyes. In the next moment her eyes went blank, as if she had pulled down a shade over her mind.

Gaia straightened. "Any other damage?" she asked, making it sound casual.

His lips tightened. "No. No other damage."

Turning back to her locker, Gaia stuffed in her puffy ski jacket, holding it in place with one hand while strategically slamming the locker shut with the other. Bedraggled feathers whisked into the air and swirled crazily before floating downward.

That was it, Ed realized. That would be the sum of her response to his almost getting killed. Some friend she was. Anger rushed through his veins, making him feel flushed and reckless and mean.

"Going to Mary's funeral on Wednesday?"

For a split second Gaia froze. If Ed had blinked, he would have missed it. It wasn't quite the gratifying response he had hoped for.

"God, no," came Gaia's reply. Then she tied her avocado green wool sweater around her waist and hitched up her books.

131

Angrily Ed pushed against her jean-clad hip. "Get out of my way," he snapped, then looked up in surprise at Gaia's sharply indrawn breath. She pulled back away from him, breathing tightly.

"I'm not in your way," she said. She turned and walked in the other direction, moving slowly and deliberately, not looking back.

Ed spun away, rolling down the hall fast. This day had, in fact, just gotten worse.

"HEATHER, IT'LL BE GREAT," MEGAN said. She leaned forward to get closer to the industrial mirror attached to the school's second-floor bathroom wall. At the row of five white, matching sinks, she occupied the last one. An open makeup bag was propped by the pitted silver cold-water handle.

She Had a Lover

"Look, first dinner at Dojo's," Megan went on. "Then we could hit Melody's and see who's playing. Come on. Don't stand us up for Phoebe again."

Heather peered at herself in her own mirror. She took a tiny dab of gloss and smoothed it over her sable brown eyebrows, making them shiny and perfectly shaped.

"Sorry, no can do," she said.

Megan paused and regarded her friend. "Heather, you hardly come out with us anymore." she complained.

Yeah, and you probably spent close to two hundred bucks last weekend, thought Heather. *Sorry, but I don't think my allowance will really cover that.* She smeared a dab of olive shadow in the crease of her lid, then redid her raisin-colored lip stain.

"So what are you doing today that you can't come with us?" Megan asked, her jaw set. She turned and crossed her arms over her chest.

Heather looked at her. She and Megan had been friends for six years, ever since junior high at Brearly. They used to be able to tell each other practically anything. Heather remembered long, sleepless nights spent at Heather's family's summer house, where the girls would stay up, eating, talking, and laughing until the sun came up.

But now everything was different. Megan's life had continued on normally. Her parents had gotten divorced, but that was no biggie. Practically everyone's parents did, sooner or later. Her mom had gotten remarried. Her father had moved to France. All that meant was that now Megan had fabulous summers in Europe while Heather sweltered in the city.

"I went with you to Ozzie's on Friday," Heather pointed out.

Megan rolled her eyes. "That was *Friday*. Now, why can't you come tonight?"

"As it so happens, I'm seeing Sam," said Heather, unable to keep the triumph out of her voice. Sam was the one big status symbol she still had, that she could still flaunt.

Sure enough, Megan looked impressed. "I thought you guys were doing the on-again, off-again thing."

"We're on again," Heather said with a shrug. "I'm going over there now to hang out, and maybe we'll grab a pizza."

"Well, good," said Megan. "I'm glad he's decided to surface."

Heather nodded. "He's been studying like crazy." She tucked in her shirt and smoothed it down over her hips. Then she rubbed the tops of her black loafers on the backs of her chinos to shine up the tops. "But I finally said, 'Sam, you have to make time for us, too, you know.'"

"What did he say?" Megan asked.

"He apologized," Heather said, a coy smile playing around her lips. "He said I was right. And he blew off a bunch of stuff so we could be together today."

"Cool."

There it was. The envious tone was back in Megan's voice. God, that sounded so good.

Heather felt very cheerful and generous. She put a hand on Megan's shoulder and gave her a warm smile. "Don't give up on me, okay?" she said lightly. "I definitely want to hang with you guys. It's just I need to see Sam, too."

"Oh, sure, of course," said Megan, all her irritation gone. She smiled slyly. "You need to keep him happy."

Heather laughed, feeling cool and sophisticated: She had a lover. A college guy lover. She was *Heather Gannis*, and for a few moments she could forget about everything: Phoebe, her parents, and even Sam's frustrating flakiness. Right at this moment everything was perfect.

WORDLESSLY GAIA MOVED HER ROOK

Blitz to bishop's seven, then glanced up into Zolov's face. Zolov looked older than dirt today; a week's worth of straggly white whiskers blurred the edges of his face, and his threadbare trench coat was streaked with something that looked like motor oil. His eyes were deeply sunken, his wrinkles more sharply defined. The cold air had chapped his skin and lips and now whipped through the sparse, whitish gray hair on his hatless head. Last week he'd had a maroon polyester knit cap. Gaia wondered what had happened to it.

Zolov considered the board for long minutes. One hand in a fingerless glove stroked his rough chin as he pondered. In the months Gaia had been hanging out among the chess junkies in Washington Square Park, Zolov was the closest thing to an international grand master that she'd seen. Despite being homeless, despite his ragged clothes, unkempt hair, and sour, permeating body smell, still, he was a truly brilliant player, and Gaia had learned some interesting middle game forms from him.

She waited impatiently for him to make his move. It was twilight in the park, that strange half hour between day and night when it was difficult to see clearly. The overhead lamps had just flickered on, casting their sickly yellow-gray glow over the snow-flecked asphalt and the concrete benches where they sat. After school Gaia had gone first to Tompkins Square Park, then here, trolling every path, making perimeter checks, until she was sure Skizz wasn't around. Today the plan was to simply hang here until she couldn't stay awake any longer. She had spotted Skizz on Saturday and had dragged herself back to the park yesterday only to strike out again. It was enough to make her scream. If she *wasn't* looking for Skizz, he'd probably be in her face every twenty minutes for some reason or another. Now she was sitting on this frozen bench, killing time by playing Zolov. Her leg and hip were aching with a deep, painful throb that made her whole being coil with tension. Okay, she would stay here till midnight, then go back to the Nivens' and soak in a hot bath. Just the thought of sinking into the steamy water was enough to make her almost moan.

Zolov reached out with one gnarled hand and carefully moved his king to king's three. On the sidelines his red Power Ranger stood steadfast. The Power Ranger was Zolov's talisman—something he was never without, something he guarded fiercely. Gaia had seen Zolov asleep on a park bench, with the tiny feet of the plastic Power Ranger tucked into the ratty scarf looped around his neck.

Sitting back, Zolov hacked a couple of times, a hollow, rattling sound coming from his concave chest. As she examined the board, Gaia wondered if Zolov had pneumonia.

Then, like a computer, Gaia's mind raced forward, seeing all the different possibilities, the different permutations of play. Her blue eyes widened as she saw Zolov's fatal flaw. It couldn't be. He had goofed. With that one move he had sentenced himself to a sure loss. They might play this game out for another hour, but the end was now certain. Gaia would win. It was amazing.

For five minutes Gaia reran the possibilities in her

mind. She came to the same conclusion. It was mate for Zolov, all the way around. Calmly she sat there, frozen and sore, and waited for Zolov to see it too.

It took him another minute. Then his wild, inch-long silver brows wrinkled and came together. His dark eyes stared at the board. He hacked a couple of times. Still Gaia sat. When she was sure Zolov knew the outcome, she reached out a hand still clad in one of George's leather gloves and gently knocked over his king.

Zolov stared at her. Then slowly he reached into the tattered pocket of his filthy coat. He withdrew a twenty-dollar bill and pushed it across the table as if it caused him physical pain to do so. Gaia wouldn't insult him by refusing to take it.

She stood up, stretched, and pocketed the twenty. "Later, Zolov," she said, trying not to groan as her injured hip screamed in protest at her movement. "Good game."

Zolov nodded, looking confused, and quickly righted his king. Behind Gaia a guy in a plaid shirt and shiny satin baseball jacket moved forward to take her place.

Gaia moved away, forcing herself not to feel pain, forcing her walk to be smooth and fluid. Forcing herself not to worry about Zolov. Never show weakness. Never show fear. Gaia knew she couldn't show fear if she tried. When she was younger, she had spent long hours in front of a mirror, trying to form her face into a mask of fear. Eyes wide, mouth opened in an O, the most she had managed was sort of a look of surprise. Even dismay, perhaps. But the blue eyes staring back at her from the mirror had never managed to register fear. And never would.

On the corner of Waverly and University Place there was a hot dog vendor, and Gaia bought herself some dinner: one large dog with the works, one Coke. Mary had always gotten a hot dog with just mustard and relish. She'd loved yellow mustard, insisting it was one of the four food groups. She had drunk diet Coke. She had also introduced Gaia to Pellegrino. Mary had been full of contradictions.

Gaia walked down Waverly on the outside of the park, eating her hot dog. *Come on, Skizz. Why don't you show soon? I need this to be over. I need to have this behind me. I can't keep thinking about this thing I'm going to do. Once you're dead, I can move on.*

An uncomfortable thought came to Gaia as she tossed her hot dog wrapper in a trash can. Move on to what? What waited for her on the other side of Skizz's death? What did she have to look forward to? What purpose would her life have afterward?

Just don't think about it.

I know Ed thinks I'm being a total jerk. But there's nothing I can do about that. He thinks I don't care about him. But I simply can't *allow* myself to care about him.

Take today, for instance: If I had time, I'd be really upset about his getting mugged at knifepoint. I'd want to hear details. I might even want to try to track the guy down and take him apart for hurting my friend. If I had time, the thought of his being alone and scared while he was being mugged would really hurt me inside. And now, when he's obviously angry at me, I'd want to try to work it out with him.

Not only that, but I might even mention that I sort of got hit by a curb on Saturday and have a humongous, black bruise from my waist practically down to my knee, and every time I take a step, I feel like the bone is going to snap in two. Then he

would fuss over me and be all
concerned.

But I can't do that right now.
I just have to get through the
next few days and look for Skizz.
That's the total agenda.

Then I'm gone.

With an odd,
tortured
expression
on his face
Sam
hesitated,
then bent
his head and
met her lips.

a
useful
skill

TOM WATCHED GAIA DISAPPEAR

around the corner of Waverly and MacDougal. Her hands were stuffed into the pockets of that ugly jacket, and she was leaving a wispy trail of gray feathers behind her, as if she carried within her a personal snowstorm that occasionally burst free.

A Hard Game

The overwhelming impulse to follow her tightened Tom Moore's gut. Cupping his hands, Tom held them to his mouth and blew on them, trying to warm them. He checked his watch, which could give him the current local times of any of a dozen countries. Here in New York, it was almost precisely five-thirty. Time to meet his contact.

Across the street from Washington Square Park was a long row of brick town houses that dated back to the mid-1800s. Most of them now belonged to NYU and housed various offices and student resources. Tom tightened the belt of his midnight blue trench coat, grateful for its cashmere lining, and crossed the street, dodging between two taxis. At five-thirty on the dot, he was quickly mounting the worn and cracked marble steps of number twelve. The brass plaque to the right of the heavy glass door said French Students Union. Tom pushed open the door and went in.

Inside, threadbare maroon carpeting dulled the

sound of his footsteps as he headed up the uneven staircase. On the fourth floor was a series of doors. Tom walked unerringly to the last one on the left, then turned to check the hall for visitors. It was quiet and deserted. He knocked four times, then twice, then once. A buzzer opened the electronic lock, and Tom pushed open the door.

"Hello, Tom," said George. "Right on time."

"George," said Tom, extending his hand. He loosened his coat and sat in the leather armchair across from his old friend. He rubbed one cold hand across his face, then took a deep breath. "I just saw her," he said, his face looking older than its forty-two years.

George nodded, gave a smile that didn't reach his eyes. "You probably see her more than I do," he said without humor.

"I'm worried about her," Tom said unnecessarily.

"We all are," George replied. "But you trained her too well, my friend. She's hard to keep up with."

Tom couldn't stop the look of paternal pride on his face.

George pushed a manila folder across the table. "We've received intelligence that Loki's interest in our girl has taken on a new twist. There's reason to believe that he wants her—for himself."

Tom's blue eyes, a darker, more clouded color than his daughter's, glanced up sharply. "But why?"

George looked uncomfortable. "You probably know Loki better than almost anyone, Tom. What does your instinct tell you? Why would he want her?"

A small muscle in Tom's jaw twitched, and a slow-burning fire seemed to fill his gaze. "I'll kill him first."

"Take a number," George said dryly. "Lots of people want Loki dead."

Tom paused and stared intently at his friend. "I have another favor to ask, George. This friend of Gaia's that was killed. Mary Moss. The papers said it was some kind of drug hit. Is that true?"

"It looks like the reports are legit," George replied, his body slackening against the chair. "The poor girl was apparently a recovering coke addict. They found drugs on the body."

"I'm worried about Gaia," Tom continued. "I'm worried she might try to go after the dealer. Can you find out some information on him for me? Anything I can use to track him down?"

"Of course," George said, nodding, "I'll do what I can."

"When's our next meeting scheduled?" For Tom and probably George, too, work was a sure refuge. By focusing on `details, protocols, expected outcomes, and failure rates,` he could avoid talking or sometimes even thinking about pain, loss, betrayal, or loneliness. It was a useful skill.

"YOU WANT SOME TEA OR SOMETHING?"

What a Hottie

Sam gestured at the small electric kettle perched on a white plastic milk crate. "I've got some hot chocolate here somewhere."

Heather laughed, wrinkling her nose. "Sam. I'm not a child," she said, giving him a look that said he of all people should know better.

He laughed, too, and ran a hand through his wonderful goldish brownish reddish hair. Heather felt a pang. Why were they still so bizarrely uncomfortable with each other? They had been going out for nine months! But they were still unsure and awkward around each other, as if they had just met.

"You want a beer, then? There's some in Mike's fridge. Or water?"

"Sam." Heather bunched up Sam's pillows against the cinder-block wall. She edged back on his bed so she was half reclining. "I'm fine. I don't need anything. Except you. Now, come here." She patted the rough wool army blanket that covered Sam's narrow bed.

In this small room Heather almost felt that she and Sam could make a connection. This was where they spent their alone time, this was where they made love.

Sam looked uncomfortable as he came and perched on the side of the bed. "Heather, I—we need to talk," he said.

147

"Can we talk later?" she asked, sliding her hand up the rumpled sleeve of his shirt.

"Um," Sam said, not looking at her. "It's just that I've been thinking, and . . . well, I was wondering where we were going with this, and—"

Heather put one finger against his mouth. "Shhh," she whispered. "Later." Then she leaned forward and gently put her mouth over his. He was unyielding for a moment, hesitant. But she put her arms around him and pressed herself close. His hands on her arms held her in place, and he moved his mouth away.

"Heather, wait—there's something I wanted to say to you."

"Oh, Sam," she whispered. "Can't it wait?" She looked deep into his eyes. "I haven't seen you in ages. I *need* you." He smelled so good—he always did. Like laundry detergent and snow and himself.

She leaned close again. "Kiss me," she asked softly. "Kiss me, Sam."

With an odd, tortured expression on his face Sam hesitated, then bent his head and met her lips. She curled her arms around him and leaned backward, pulling him down with her.

Sam's arm came around her waist, and Heather felt the familiar, thrilling tingle that being close to Sam always produced. They'd had a lot of ups and downs—she'd been unfaithful to him with Charlie

Salita; he'd admitted that he was obsessed with Gaia Moore. But here they were, together and alone, and Heather desperately wanted to love him and have him love her. If she could have just one thing in her life that was certain, strong, constant . . . it would make everything else all right. She curled her left hand around his neck and pressed closer to him.

God, she loved kissing. Not that she had kissed that many people. Ever since eighth grade Heather had been so popular that she could afford to be picky and, in fact, had an obligation to be picky, to be hard to get. There were standards to set.

She hadn't even gone to third base until her first real serious boyfriend, Ed Fargo. And since Ed there had been only Sam. Heather was working hard on forgetting that Charlie Salita had ever happened. Thank God, Sam had never found out about that disastrous mistake. She had been com- pletely falling-down drunk, she had been angry at Sam, she had been furious with Gaia, and she had ended up going into a bedroom with a gorgeous hunk from her school. She still didn't know if she had agreed to have sex with Charlie or whether he had raped her. The whole thing was so horrible, she just couldn't think about it. *Focus on Sam.*

"Mmm," she hummed under her breath as he

pressed closer. They were kissing slowly, without urgency, more cuddling and smooching than getting hot and heavy. It was really nice, just what she needed. She slipped her hand under his shirt in back, gliding up over the smooth skin. She didn't even remember Charlie, didn't remember anything but kissing him. She had no idea how he had felt or if she had liked it or hated it. Which was good. The less she remembered the better, right? The easier it should be to block it out.

"Heather," Sam said, pulling back a bit.

She smiled up at him and shifted so she could pull her shirt out from her waistband. Sam was always so gentle, so loving. He always cared about her feelings, never made her feel like it was just physical. She took his hand and pushed it under her shirt in back. She pressed against him, her breasts flattening against his chest. She wriggled a little against him.

He drew in a shaky breath.

He was nothing like Ed. When she and Ed had lost their virginity together, well, the first time had been so amazing. They knew what they were supposed to do but didn't realize it might be physically difficult, especially on a sandy beach. It had been pretty uncomfortable for her, and she had cried while he held her. Once she had gotten used to it, it had still been so awkward and weird and new that

150

they had both been amazed, awestruck. She had been almost crazy with love for him, this reckless skate rat who was so different from her other friends.

After that very first time they had been wild for each other, sneaking chances to be together whenever they could. It had been summertime, and their skins would be sweaty and slick and smooth as they moved together, delight written on their faces. Ed had been strong, inventive, funny, and intense in bed, and sometimes, when he was looking deep into her eyes and she could feel him against her, their connection had been so mind-blowing that tears had come to her eyes. *This is it,* she had thought. *This is what I want for the rest of my life.*

Then there had been the horrible accident that left Ed paralyzed from the waist down. Heather and Ed had gone from the highest high to the lowest low in about twenty seconds, and they had never recovered.

Months after they had broken up, Heather had met Sam. Sam had practically saved her life; he'd made her happy again. All her friends went from feeling sorry for her to envying her. It had been great.

Heather stroked her fingers through Sam's soft, wavy hair as he lowered his head and began to unbutton her shirt. He kissed her neck, under her chin, then began to trail a line of kisses down her throat as he undid buttons one by one. Ed's hair had been thick and straight, dark as coffee. It had brushed against her stomach as he . . . oh, Ed.

Sam raised his head. "What?" he asked.

She stared at him dumbly. "Huh?"

"Did you say something?" Sam's hazel eyes were heavy lidded, his mouth smooth and kissable.

Heather shook her head. "Uh . . ."

Waiting, Sam hovered over her chest, his hands holding the two edges of her shirt. Suddenly, with no warning, Heather felt yucky. As if Sam had just turned into Charlie Salita. What a bizarre thought. She must be losing her mind. All she knew was that she suddenly just wanted to go home.

"You okay?" Sam smiled softly, stroking her.

"Oh, jeez, Sam, I forgot!" Heather said inanely. She sat up and buttoned her shirt as quickly as she could with trembling fingers.

"What? Forgot what?"

"I'm supposed to go home for dinner tonight!" Heather blurted out. She stood up shakily, wondering where she'd put her shoes. "I'm sorry, Sam. I told Mom I had a date with you, but . . . ," she blathered on, conscious of Sam's uncomprehending stare as she shoved her feet into her shoes, grabbed her purse and her bag, and tore out of Sam's room like it was on fire.

SAM SAT ON HIS BED, LOOKING AT

His Tortured Sex Life

his half-open door for who knew how long after Heather had left. He was a . . . what was the word? A dog? All the things that described him seemed so old-fashioned, like they were from a forties movie. A cad, a rotter, a heel. The only modern word he could think of was *dog*, and that seemed so . . . harsh somehow. Better just to call him a loser.

How else to describe a guy who was making out with his girlfriend, the girlfriend he was determined to break up with, while fantasizing about another girl, a girl who hated him, a girl who had totally shot him down the last time he saw her? Instead of Heather's rich dark hair Sam had seen a blond, tangled sprawl across his pillow. Instead of Heather's neat, curvy little body Sam had felt long legs, a firm, flat belly, strong arms holding him tightly to her.

"Yo! Moon Man!" Mike Suarez barged in through the open door. "You eaten yet?"

Sam wordlessly shook his head.

"Come on! It's Italian night over at Weinstein!" Mike pounded the door with a closed fist, sign of an excess of testosterone. Sam leaned over and methodically put on his hiking boots. Their dorm didn't have its own dining room—to eat, they had to go to Rubin or Weinstein dorms or to Loeb center. A bitch when it was cold and snowing and when you had just sunk to a new low.

Mike and Sam headed out and started trotting down the four flights of stairs to the lobby. It was official: Sam was an asshole. Once Heather started kissing him and moving against him, he'd lost the will to break up with her. His mind knew what he had to do, but his body had refused to listen. How weak was that? Compared with his tortured and convoluted sex life, his premed classes were a walk in the park.

"I'M BORRRRED." ED TRIED TO PUT

Ed 'n' Heather

as much anguished whining into his voice as possible. On the other end of the phone Heather giggled, then stopped and cleared her throat.

"Ed, it's a Monday night," she said briskly. "Go do your homework."

"Done." He waited. Why had he called Heather? Well, who else did he have to call? It's not like he had a best friend or anything. It's not like anyone else was calling *him*. Given a choice between phoning his ex-girlfriend, whom he was now sort of friends with again, and sitting around at home in a **vegetative state**, wondering what the hell Gaia was up to, he had chosen calling his ex.

"Watch TV," was Heather's next suggestion.

"TV rots your mind," was Ed's opinion. "What are you doing?"

"Oh, well, you know . . . the usual." That sounded pretty lame.

"Have you eaten yet?"

"Actually, no. I just got in. I'm starving."

Ed's spirits brightened. "Me too. Look, why don't I stop at Ray's, pick up a pizza, and bring it over? We'll hang out, we'll eat . . ."

"I shouldn't admit this," Heather said dryly, "but that's the best offer I've had all day."

Ed didn't give her a chance to change her mind. "See you in a few."

IT HAD BEEN A LONG TIME SINCE

The Gannis Homestead

Heather had seen Ed eating in her kitchen. He still ate with gusto. She watched him demolish his third piece of pizza while she toyed with the crust of her first.

Ed's dark eyes focused on her plate. "Don't tell me you're dieting," he said warningly.

"No, no," Heather said, cutting herself another half slice. She took a bite.

"Good, because I hate that crap," said Ed. "If you went on a diet, you'd shrivel up and blow away. And you look good the way you are."

Silently Heather hoped Phoebe wasn't anywhere near the kitchen. Her cheeks warmed at Ed's compliment. It had been ages since she'd thought of him in *that* way. Well, it *had* been ages, until this afternoon, when she had been with Sam. Now she looked at Ed across the table, the way his dark hair fell across his forehead, his broad shoulders, broader and heavier now with muscle, his arms and strong, lean hands. Even that big cut across her cheek didn't detract from his good looks.

"Ed, how sexist of you," she said sweetly. "Next you'll start talking about big boobs and wide, child-bearing hips."

Across the table Ed grinned evilly at her. "More cush to the push."

Her eyes widened in outrage, and she threw a piece of crust at him. "What a pig! No wonder you don't have a girlfriend!"

Deflecting the crust, Ed snickered. "You think that's it?"

"Hello, Ed!" said Mr. Gannis with forced heartiness.

He came into the kitchen and opened the fridge. "You're looking well."

"Thanks. You too," Ed said easily. Heather grimaced to herself.

"What are you kids doing tonight?" Mr. Gannis asked cheerfully, popping the top of a beer bottle. He slowly poured it into a pint glass. Ed watched the foam build.

Shrugging, Heather said, "Watching a movie?"

"Well, honey, you know tonight's the State of the Union Address," Mr. Gannis said. "Your mother and I were planning to watch it. Maybe you kids could hang out in your room so we won't disturb you."

"Sure, whatever," said Heather. "Come on, Shred. Unless you want to watch the State of the Union report with Dad."

"Oh, no, thanks," Ed said.

Heather hid a smirk as she watched Ed expertly push back from the table and head down the hall to her room. Of course he still remembered where it was.

Inside her room, he looked around, assessing changes.

"Different posters," he said.

"Yeah," she said, flopping sideways on her bed. Ed's face looked very still—no longer lighthearted and open, the way it had been earlier.

"What's wrong?" Heather asked. "I know that look."

Surprise crossed his face, then he shook his head. "I'm just . . . It's just insulting, that's all."

"What is?" Frowning, Heather ran through everything she had said in the last twenty minutes. Had she hurt his feelings somehow?

"Look, if I wasn't in a wheelchair, there's no way your dad would have suggested we come hang out in here," Ed burst out. "Before, I'd have had to crawl over his dead body to get into your room. Now it's like, sure, go in, you . . . eunuch!"

Heather felt shocked, and she realized he was right. It was as if her dad considered Ed absolutely no threat to her virtue, like he was one of her girlfriends. It *was* insulting. Why, Ed had been more threat to her virtue than anyone she'd ever met!

"*Eunuch*," Heather said admiringly. "Someone's been doing his English homework. That's a mighty fancy word."

She saw Ed's hands clench on his wheel rims as he stared at her in angry disbelief. Quickly she scooted to the edge of her bed and leaned toward Ed.

"Let Daddy think what he wants," she said softly. "I like having you in here."

Interesting, she thought as she watched Ed's pupils dilate.

This situation is starting to prey on my brain. I didn't see Skizz again last night. I'm going to end up with pneumonia if I keep freezing my butt off like this.

On top of that, when I got home, the Wicked Witch of the West Village was waiting for me, chain smoking and knocking back gin and tonics. The alcohol fumes almost knocked me down when I opened the front door.

The weird thing was, she didn't say a word. Just stared at me with those acidic green eyes as smoke coiled around her flame red hair. I waited for her to start in on me, but she just bored holes in me with her eyes as I trudged up the stairs. I didn't see George—I hope I don't find him buried in the backyard soon.

You know what? I feel very tired. Last night I wanted to just lie down in the snow and fall asleep. I'm tired of looking for Skizz, though I won't stop.

I'm tired of tensing up every time I have to go back to Perry Street. My hip is still killing me. My whole thigh is mottled black and purple and deep blue, with tinges of green and yellow around the edges. Very artistic.

Okay, here's my fantasy. Some night soon I find Skizz. Quickly, without thinking about it, I finish what I've decided to do. Then I go home, stopping for a box of chocolate Krispy Kreme doughnuts on the way. I take the doughnuts into the bathroom and run a deep tub of water as hot as I can stand it. I set a fluffy white towel, two cans of Coke, and a bottle of Advil on a little table. I sink into the water. I take four Advil pills and drink a Coke. I eat three doughnuts. I drink another Coke. I fall asleep.

No one calls me, no one comes in, no one needs the bathroom. When I finally get out of the tub, glowing pinkly and shriveled

like a prune, Ella tells me I've
been kicked out of the Village
School and am being transferred
to another foster home in, say,
France. I never have to see anything that reminds me of Mary
again. I never see Ed again,
never have to explain anything to
him. And best of all, someone
else is planning it all for me.

I eat another doughnut as I
pack.

That would be the perfect day
for me.

It's not too much for a girl
to ask, is it?

Every twenty
minutes
someone **perfect**
was having
sex, and it **day**
wasn't Gaia.

THE ONLY GOOD THING ABOUT TUESDAYS, in Gaia's opinion, was that they weren't Mondays. Mondays were so awful, it was like a blow to the head. Tuesdays were more of a dull, achy pounding.

Well, Shit

As Gaia determinedly pushed her stack of textbooks back in her locker, she caught sight of Ed turning the corner at the end of the hall. Probably she should say hello to him. She'd been a little harsh, although she'd meant what she said. But she could at least be civil. It was just—in her mind, she had already crossed a line. She had left him behind as surely as if she'd already skipped town. There was no explaining it or justifying it to him. And it was too late to change her mind.

But today she wanted to at least be nice to him. Try to make him see that she didn't hate him, no matter what it looked like. Say a simple *hello*, and keep on moving. Maybe one day he would understand that it was for his own good.

Before Gaia could take a step in Ed's direction, her archenemy, Heather Gannis, stepped into view. Strangely, Heather slithered up to Ed and squeezed his shoulder. One side of her mouth quirked. Gaia moved forward, waiting for Ed to push Heather's hand away and roll past her.

But no. Ed smiled boyishly, suddenly looking younger and charming. Even adorable. Gaia stopped as if she had been poleaxed.

"I had such a good time last night," Heather said.

Her stomach clenching, Gaia leaned against the bank of lockers. Had she woken up to an alternate universe? She knew that Ed and Heather had been involved once, though she hated to think about it. And she knew they were civil to each other now, though the reasoning escaped her. But what the hell was *this* about?

"Me too," said Ed, grinning. His dark eyes looked up into Heather's, and something unnamable passed between them. Then the bell rang, and Ed continued down the hall. Gaia pasted a sardonic look on her face and loped forward, already formulating the kind of crap she would give Ed about his recent lapse in good taste.

Before she could open her mouth, Ed calmly said, "Hey, Gaia." Then he rolled right past her without looking back, leaving her gaping at him like a goldfish on a sidewalk. For a moment Gaia closed her eyes and rubbed one hand over her lids. She definitely needed more sleep, more Advil, more coffee. She would need all the help she could get to deal with this bizarre and disturbing development.

IN CHEM LAB HEATHER PUSHED HER

Lah-de-dah

goofy safety glasses up onto her shining dark hair, managing to look both chic and careless. She caught sight of her reflection in one of the glass-fronted cupboards that lined the back of the room and smiled at herself.

As she and her lab partner, Megan, set up their Bunsen burners and their stupid little asbestos pads and their beakers that would have been so much more appealing if they had held frozen margaritas (no salt), `Heather couldn't remember the last time she had felt so happy.`

"Well, *you're* glowing," Megan said accusingly under her breath. In the front of the room Mr. Fowler droned on about chemical reaction this and mechanical reaction that, but he was easy to tune out. Gaia Moore, however, was not. She came into the room looking like an oversized refugee, as usual, and took her place two desks away.

"You and Sam must have gotten along well," said Megan knowingly. "*Really* well."

Seeing Gaia's back stiffen almost imperceptibly, Heather wanted to burst into song.

"It was really nice," Heather said demurely. "Sometimes just being alone with him is all I need."

Megan snorted in an `unladylike` way. "Were you there until late?"

For once Heather appreciated Megan's usually annoying habit of speaking a tiny bit too loud. Obviously Gaia was overhearing every word. It was *delicious*. What better way to celebrate Heather's happiness than by twisting a knife right in Gaia's guts? Call her sentimental.

Heather shook her head. "No—I got home pretty early. Then Ed came over, and we hung out in my room."

Megan gaped at her. From the corner of Heather's eye she saw Gaia's head turning toward her, as if someone were pulling a string.

"Ed Fargo?" Megan squealed. She took off her safety glasses to stare at Heather.

"Ed and I are good friends," Heather said calmly, lighting their Bunsen burner. "Really good friends."

"You hung out in your room? Your dad let him into your room?"

Stifling a giggle, Heather nodded. "What Dad doesn't know won't hurt him," she said mischievously.

"You and Ed . . ." Megan seemed at a loss for words. "And Sam?"

"I had a very full day yesterday," Heather allowed. Then she turned right toward Viking Girl and smiled big, catching Gaia by surprise.

"I had forgotten how *great* Ed is," Heather said breathily. She actually winked at Gaia, even though she didn't think she had ever winked at anyone in her life. The response was intensely satisfying: Gaia looked startled, repulsed, confused, and angry all at once. Heather wrinkled her nose at Gaia in a girlish way, then turned back and busily started her experiment. Life was good when you were Heather Gannis.

BY THE TIME TRIG CLASS WAS HALF

over, Gaia still hadn't recovered from the sharp nosedive her world had taken in the last two hours. For some reason, dealing with the gross **Boinking Like Weasels**

unfairness of losing both her parents early in her life was one thing: She could somehow wrap her mind around it and try to function. But the idea of wretched, horrible, fakey bitch Heather Gannis having both Sam Moon and Ed Fargo drooling over her was more than Gaia could stand.

Sure, Heather was gorgeous. The glossy dark hair, the uptilted hazel green eyes, the peaches 'n' cream skin. And she was a normal height, and she had girlie curves. Her sweaters actually had stuff to cling to. She wasn't gargantuan, muscled like a truck driver, awkward, and mannish. But so what? Did that make it fair?

In all of Gaia's seventeen years she had only ever desired one person, and *Heather* was having sex with him on a regular basis. In the last five years she had been friends with only two people. One was dead, and Heather was friends with, and possibly having sex with, the other one. How unfair was that?

And what was this, with all these people boinking like weasels all the time? Every twenty minutes someone was having sex, and it wasn't Gaia. In her whole life she had been kissed romantically exactly *four times,* and one she wasn't sure about, one was Charlie Salita because she was luring him into a trap, and the last one was with Ed on a freaking *dare!* Only one time had actually been fun, and that had been with a random guy in a club. This was just so lame. Mary had been right. Gaia was clearly a case of arrested development. In the romance department. Not in the martial arts/muscles/nerves-of-steel departments.

Gaia suddenly felt unbearably hurt. And she hadn't thought it was possible to hurt any more than she already did. Usually, no matter what happened, she just kept on moving. Kept her head up. This time last year it didn't matter that she was alone, that she had no friends, that she had only herself to depend on. Why should it matter now?

Gaia shook her head, keeping her eyes cast down

on the meaningless trig equations in front of her. She was lost and spinning and didn't know what to do with herself. If she could have felt fear, this would be a good time. Because she couldn't, all she could feel was a sort of nausea.

TODAY'S MENU: CORNED BEEF HASH (no doubt Alpo brand), creamed corn, steamed spinach, and a square of spice cake. Groaning, Ed decided to grab some falafel at Falafel King, only a block and a half away. Yes, it was cold outside. Yes, he would have to negotiate snowdrifts and piles of garbage. But he couldn't eat this swill, and a lad had to keep up his strength.

Slow Burn

As he swiveled and headed out the cafeteria, he saw Gaia standing in line. Her eyes caught his, and she looked away. He smiled to himself as he remembered the scene in the hallway this morning. That had been fun. Gaia had looked so pissed. Now he kept his eyes on her as she looked away. Was he mistaken, or was she doing a slow burn? Did she want him now that she probably thought Heather did? Not that Heather really did, of course: Despite hanging out with Ed last night, she was still together with Sam, as far as Ed knew.

So in reality Ed was still girlfriendless, loverless. But he knew it looked to Gaia like that might have changed, with Heather. Hee hee.

He stopped in front of Gaia. As usual, despite the scowl on her face, she looked beautiful. She and Heather were so different: Heather was groomed, sophisticated, and sexy in this confident, self-aware way. Gaia was always a mess, completely unsophisticated, and sexy in a way that was all the more devastating because she seemed so unaware of it. Heather looked like she was ready to be led to bed. Gaia looked like she had just gotten out of it. It was enough to make a guy postal.

"Hey," Ed said.

"Hey," Gaia responded without looking at him.

It was ridiculous, but Ed felt so confident, he felt like it wouldn't kill him to forgive her—to make one last try.

"Want to go grab some falafel at Falafel King?"

A nanosecond of indecision crossed Gaia's perfect face.

She shook her head. "No, thanks."

This was so stupid. "Gaia—"

"What?" she said, looking at him finally. Irritation had bloomed in her voice. Her blue eyes were cold.

You know what? He didn't need this. Shaking his head abruptly, Ed wheeled away.

Okay. Here's my new fantasy. I still kill Skizz. I still get the doughnuts. But on my way home to the hot bath, I see Heather, Sam, and Ed all get hit by a bus. Only Ed makes it. And it isn't so bad for him because he's *already* in a wheelchair. He begs my forgiveness for five years. I'm not sure if I ever give in.

So some guy calls—my private cell, no less. Says a friend of a friend told him I got the shit. You a cop? I said. He laughed. Named some names no cop knows. So I know he's legit—just some asshole with a hungry nose. I say meet me at midnight. He begs. Big party, boring people, really needs it sooner. I've heard that story a million times. Anyway, he begs and promises. So I haul my sorry ass out of bed, do a couple of lines like a quality control check. Take some of them pain pills the hospital gave me. Ready to roll. So I'm heading to the corner of frigging Waverly and MacDougal, and it's light out, and I'm gonna be a frigging sitting duck. Asshole better not let me down.

SKIZZ

The
familiar,
heady rush
of **positively**
adrenaline
poured **insane**
like whiskey
through her
veins.

"I'M TELLING YOU, YOU'VE GOT

Out of Her Misery

to get me out of there." Ella's voice was brittle. She lifted her heavy crystal tumbler of gin and tonic and took a healthy, if unladylike, swig.

"Your job is unfinished." Loki sounded completely unconcerned with her mental state. He sat behind a smooth black desk, its top bare except for the heavy manila file he was leafing through. The room was silent except for the ice tinkling in Ella's glass and the occasional muted turning of papers.

"Forget the job," Ella said rashly, and was rewarded with Loki's icy stare. She took a breath and forced herself to calm down. "Look, I've been doing it for a long time," she reminded him. "I can't take living with that—that horrible sack of *laundry* another day. You've no idea what it's like. I can't bear it." She ached for a cigarette with a palpable longing. With one red-clawed fingertip she smeared the trace of lipstick left on her glass.

"You'll bear it because I say you have to," Loki said quietly, calmly.

Ella was upset and angry and fed up, but she wasn't stupid. Her danger-sensing antenna prickled, and once again she told herself to calm down.

"It's just very frustrating," she said more reasonably. "George is *repugnant*. If I have to let him touch me one more time—" She took a deep breath. "And that girl. I know you think she's hot stuff, but to me she's nothing but hateful, rude, and disrespectful."

Loki actually let his papers rest on his desk and looked up at her. "And that hurts your tender feelings?" he asked disbelievingly. "What does it matter how she is to you? Your *feelings* are completely immaterial in this situation. So what if old George wants a feel now and then? Lie on your back and think of England." He quoted the old saying with obvious callousness.

"You don't seem to remember," he continued softly, "that your usefulness is limited only to what information you bring me about Gaia. Your many mistakes have been overlooked, for the time being, because like it or not, you're still closer to Gaia than anyone else on our side."

Ella drained her glass and set it down, too hard, on the glass-topped coffee table. The noise it made sounded like a gunshot. Loki's face was a mask.

Silence filled the room. Once Ella had been Loki's protégée, his rising star. Now she was yesterday's socks. He had found her when she was younger than Gaia, had molded her into what she was today. But now she had the sickening feeling that he thought of her as the trial run and Gaia as the final test. But not if she could help it. She licked her lips.

"I know," she said, allowing resignation to fill her voice.

"Is she going to the Moss girl's funeral tomorrow?"

Ella shook her head. "The girl's mother called several times, asking Gaia to speak at the service. Gaia refused. She was a real bitch, in fact." She studied her nails.

Loki smiled. "What's the point of going? Gaia doesn't allow mere emotions to cloud her judgment. The girl's role in her life is over, so Gaia moves on. She's like a shark, our Gaia." As he looked out the high window, Loki's face softened almost unnoticeably. "Like a beautiful, perfectly designed shark: nature's perfect predator. . . ." His voice trailed off thoughtfully.

If Ella had to listen to any more of this, she would throw up all over the white carpeting. Instead she lurched to her feet, unsteady for a moment on her high heels. She pulled down her tight skirt and smoothed her hands over her hips. For a moment she hoped a look of sexual interest would cross Loki's carved face. When he gazed back at her impassively, she felt ashamed, angry.

Standing at the elevator bank a minute later, Ella quickly lit a cigarette, ignoring the smoke-free-building signs plastered in front of her. Her feelings felt raw. She needed some kind of balm, something that would soothe this rough, maddening itch.

Two words popped into her fevered mind. *Sam Moon.* That delicious boy. Ella inhaled her smoke deeply, drawing it down into her lungs. Already she felt her nerves unraveling, smoothing out. Okay. First she would go home and get some rest. Then she would look up her old buddy, old pal, Sam Moon.

When the elevator doors dinged open, Ella was smiling.

Mrs. Moss's Request

NO ONE USED THE HANDICAPPED-ONLY side entrance at the Village School—no one but Ed. He used to be self-conscious about it, but now he just figured, why beef about having your own private entrance and exit? It was better than being one of the lemmings.

Today Ed waited for the door to open and wheeled himself through. Cold air instantly swirled around him, insinuating itself under the collar of his coat, around the wrist cuffs of his gloves. He'd seen

Gaia striding out the front doors only moments after the last bell had rung. No doubt she was keeping another one of her stupid appointments with fate. Trying to find Skizz. Ed had wondered what she would do to Skizz when she found him. Would she . . . go all the way? She wouldn't, would she? Sure, Gaia had a warped sense of appropriate behavior, but she wasn't a killer. Was she? What was going through her head? Ed wanted to spit with frustration and anger.

He started to wheel himself down the long, sloping wooden ramp.

"Ed?" came a hesitant female voice.

Looking up in surprise, Ed saw Mary's mother standing to one side of the ramp. She looked pale, with red-rimmed eyes, and seemed about ten years older than she had over the Christmas holidays.

"Mrs. Moss," Ed said, concern creasing his forehead.

"Forgive me for tracking you down at school," Mrs. Moss said awkwardly.

"It's okay."

Having gotten his attention, Mary's mother seemed unsure how to continue. She was silent for long moments, looking uncomfortable, as Ed took in her dark green wool coat, the expensive leather gloves lined with fur. She wore no hat, and her wavy hair, once red like Mary's but now faded and streaked with white, was being tossed by the chill wind.

"Um, can I help you with something?" Ed asked gently.

"Yes," Mrs. Moss said with a rush of relief. "Yes. I hate to impose on you, but—" She twisted her hands together.

"It's okay," Ed said again. "If there's anything I can do to help . . ."

"The thing is," said Mrs. Moss, "we—my family and I—feel so strongly that Mary would have wanted Gaia to take part in her . . . services tomorrow. It was Gaia who confronted Mary about her . . . problem, and she was why Mary decided to quit."

"Uh-huh," Ed said stonily. He saw where this was going.

"I've called her several times," Mrs. Moss continued, looking almost embarrassed, "but I guess . . . maybe she's overwhelmed with grief. As we all are."

Maybe she's overwhelmed with being an asshole, Ed thought.

"Anyway. I was hoping. The services are tomorrow. I know you were planning to come, and I thank you. But—I know you're Gaia's friend—do you think there's any way you could talk to her? Ask her, as a friend, to do this for another friend? Even if . . . even if that friend is no longer here?" Mrs. Moss ended on a cracked, hoarse whisper.

Ed felt like his guts were being churned in a washing machine. Gaia was being such a bitch! How could she say no to Mary's mother? How could she be so cold to another person's pain? *Overwhelmed with grief, my ass!*

"I'm sorry you've been having a hard time getting through to her," Ed said, a rigid cord of anger threading through his voice. "She's been taking a little vacation from being human lately."

Mary's mother misunderstood. "Oh, believe me, I know," she said, forcing a thin smile. "I think we all have. This kind of thing is just too painful to bear sometimes—it hurts too much to deal with. I don't blame her at all. It's just—I know it would mean so much to Mary. And I feel that we let her—Mary—down so badly." She looked away, her eyes haunted. "I wanted to be able to do this one last thing for her."

Ed felt that if Gaia were here, he would somehow regain enough use of his legs to personally kick her perfect ass from here till next week. Seeing Mrs. Moss, with all her raw pain on display, made something snap inside Ed. Suddenly he knew the time had come to quit being put off by Gaia's rudeness, her prickliness, her deliberate jerkiness. He was going to get through to her, he was going to get her to agree to go to Mary's funeral, or he was going to beat the shit out of her and make her cry—

just as Mary's mother was crying. It didn't matter if he destroyed what was left of their friendship forever. If there was anything left at all. It didn't matter if it would totally and irrevocably ruin his chances of making her see him as a possible boyfriend. This was it.

"I understand," he told Mrs. Moss, already feeling the adrenaline racing through his veins. Despite the cold wind his skin was flushed, and he felt hot and uncomfortable. "I'll find Gaia and ask her. I'm sure she'll be there."

"Oh, Ed, do you think so?" The light of hope in her eyes was heart wrenching.

"Yes," he said, his calm voice belying the raging emotions twisting inside him. "I really do."

A Walk in the Park

ON HER WAY TO WASHINGTON SQUARE Park, her home away from home, Gaia decided to spring for a cellophane-wrapped package of five churros. Churros, in her opinion, were right up there on her list of favorite fried foods. These of course were no longer hot; Gaia had no idea when the short, dark Guatemalan vendor had fried them—perhaps this morning? But anyway. Even cold and a little stale, they were greasy, doughy, sugary, and satisfying.

The sky overhead was heavy with low, sullen clouds. They couldn't possibly be about to get more snow, could they? The paper had said that this year was a record breaker in terms of number of freezing days and amount of precipitation. It was as if the weather were responding directly to Gaia's emotions. Low and, yes, she admitted it, sullen.

Ugh, what a sucky day. Ed and Heather, Sam and Heather, mind-numbing classes, an awful lunch . . . and to top it all off, the only underwear she'd been able to find was an ancient pair with too loose elastic. She'd been hitching them up all day.

Automatically Gaia swerved to go past the chess tables. Zolov was there, still hacking as he methodically decimated the opening play of an out-of-place businessman in a thick Burberry coat. Mr. Haq was walking fast toward his taxicab, his break over, and his opponent was still staring in frustration at the unfinished game on the board. Only a couple of other hard cores were there—the crappy weather having scared off all but the most dedicated.

What was she doing here? Skizz most likely wouldn't show until late tonight. She should go home, do her homework, rest a little, then head out again and hit Tompkins Square Park as well. Okay, maybe just a quick perimeter check. Through the park to the replica of the Arc de Triomphe, take a left on Waverly, another left on MacDougal, etc., etc., etc.

WAS SHE HALLUCINATING? HAD HER

The Angel of Death

hunger to get Skizz, to make him pay for hiring Mary's hit, finally caused her mind to snap? Because it looked like the object of her quest was standing in broad daylight on the corner in front of her, down at the end of the block.

Gaia quickened her pace, her trained eyes sweeping the area for anything that might mistakenly interfere in her final meting out of justice. No mistakes this time.

Amazingly she got closer and closer, and none of her alarm antennae went off. Her boots crunched on salt chunks as she rushed down the sidewalk. Her heart sped up, her lungs began to suck in air. The familiar, heady rush of adrenaline poured like whiskey through her veins. At last she would get her hands on Skizz. She would see his skin split under her blows, feel his bones shatter. She would finish the job that Mary had stopped her from finishing almost two weeks before.

Skizz was glancing around, looking nervous and pissed. He hadn't seen her yet. What luck, what luck, what luck . . . Hands clenched inside leather gloves, injured hip seeming strong and whole, mouth already dry, Gaia moved forward: the triumphant angel of death.

Time was moving slowly, so slowly as Gaia sorted plans, actions, approaches, and filed them into her hyperexcited brain. This was it, the goal that had defined her life, had become her life, ever since Mary died on New Year's Eve. She actually smiled.

There was no going back now. Her life would never be the same.

Gaia broke into a run. She didn't want to blow it this time. She could already feel Skizz's bones breaking. She could already see the blood. She could smell it. She was glad she didn't have a gun. Using her bare hands would be so much more satisfying.

Visions flashed through Gaia's mind in time with her steps as they pounded against the pavement. Mary, her teeth stained with blood. Skizz, lying dead on the sidewalk. Her father.

Halfway across the park Gaia suddenly became aware of two things: One was that Ed was heading toward her across one of the streets that lined the park. He was moving fast, and he looked furious. How weird. The other was that a nondescript tan sedan had pulled over to the curb, and Skizz was stepping forward to meet it.

No, Gaia screamed to herself, remembering how Skizz had escaped before.

No, no, no. It felt like a recurring nightmare.

Gaia's feet pounded the sidewalk as she raced toward Skizz. As soon as she was close enough, she could bring him down in a flying tackle. . . .

But Skizz didn't get in the car. As she raced toward him, Gaia watched events unfolding one frame at a time, almost in slow motion: The darkened back window of the car rolled slowly down. The dull metal barrel of a gun peeped coyly out.

A flash of fire lit the dark interior of the car, revealing a dark shadow in silhouette. The air was filled with a deafening burst of sound. Gaia stumbled to a disbelieving halt.

Fifteen feet from her Skizz jerked oddly, his body twisted at an inhuman angle. Gaia saw a look of astonishment cross his ugly, pock-marked face. As he fell backward, he peered down at his chest, put up his hands to stem the exploding red flower blooming there. His body hit the ground like a rock. The car roared away down West Fourth Street and was gone, leaving a thin trail of foul monoxide in its wake.

Oh God, Mary. Oh God. Gaia shook herself from her stupor and sprinted toward Skizz's body. She reached him, panting, and knelt down above him.

Oh, Mary. Gaia felt every fiber of her body explode in rage. Someone had beaten her to it. Someone had taken away the only thing she'd had to hold on to. What a waste. What a senseless waste.

Wake up. Gaia found it hard to fathom that Skizz was actually dead. She desperately wanted to wake him up—she wanted his last conscious moment to be of her railing at him, avenging her friend. But his eyes were open and glassy: He'd been dead before he hit the ground.

This was it. This was the limit of what Gaia could bear. She had finally reached it. Anguish over Mary's senseless death, the pain and desolation she'd felt since then, her confusion over Ed all roiled up out of Gaia in a raw, appalling wail. Screaming with rage and despair, she balled her fists and slammed them into Skizz's chest, once, twice. Her hands came up bloody. "You bastard!" she screamed. "You bastard! You son of a bitch, you die, you hear me? You go on and die!"

A strong hand grabbed her shoulder and pulled her backward.

"Gaia, stop it!" Ed commanded her. His face looked pale and shocked.

"Get off me!" Gaia shrieked, batting his hand away. "Don't you get it? Don't you see? Skizz is dead! He killed Mary, and now he's dead! And I didn't do it! I was going to kill him, Ed," she blurted out. "I was going to kill him, and before he died, I was going to make sure he knew it was because of Mary." She drew in a choking breath. "But I didn't! I didn't do anything! Oh God! Mary, I'm sorry!"

A crowd of people had formed. From far off, Gaia heard police sirens. Her head was about to explode. Her chest felt like an ax had been buried in it. If she didn't get out of here right now, she would turn into even more of a shrieking, freaking lunatic.

Abruptly she stood up. "Dammit!" she shouted. Pulling back her right foot, she savagely kicked Skizz's dead body. "Dammit to hell!" The gathered crowd murmured in alarm.

"Gaia, for God's sake," Ed yelled. Again he pulled roughly at her, his hand slipping on her puffy nylon jacket. "Gaia! Stop it! You're not doing anything!"

Eyes wild, hair in a yellow tangle around her tragic face, Gaia stared at him. "I know," she whispered hoarsely. Then, as the sound of police sirens grew closer, she turned, gave Skizz one last glance, and ran off. In seconds she had disappeared.

Ed was ready to scream himself. Gaia had snapped. She had truly snapped, and why? Because she had been going through all this alone. Because she hadn't trusted him. Because she had shut him out. Feeling a renewed burst of anger, Ed popped a wheelie as he spun to head after her.

WHAT TO DO? WHERE TO GO? GAIA hit a jogging stride that covered ground fast. Her brain felt like it was going to burst out of her skull. Catching sight of her **Pointless** reflection in a store window, she cracked a startled grin. She looked positively insane. Her leather gloves were dark and sticky with blood, and she had a smear of it on her jacket. Her hair looked like it had been styled by a Weedwacker, and there was a look in her eyes that would have scared her if she could, you know . . . yeah.

Skizz was dead. Skizz was dead. He had died a pathetic, public, drug dealer's death on a New York sidewalk, and no one would mourn his passing. He'd probably been the target of another drug dealer or maybe a client he'd screwed over one too many times. By tomorrow the ranks of lower-level dealers would have moved up seamlessly to take over his trade and accounts, and like water closing over a sinking pebble, it would soon be impossible to tell that Skizz had ever existed, had ever taken up space on earth.

But Gaia hadn't been the cause of his death, and for that she would never forgive herself. *I'm sorry, Mary. I'm sorry.*

A car horn blaring broke into Gaia's thoughts and made her stop short. With dull surprise she noticed she was at a broad intersection far away from Washington Square Park: She almost never made it up this far, to Fourteenth Street. Fourteenth Street was as different from the Village as the Upper East Side was different from the Bowery. It was a very wide, two-way street, teeming with traffic. Big, lower-end department stores selling everything from luggage to masking tape to wall clocks featuring porcelain unicorns lined both sides of the avenue. In between the stores were tiny cubbies selling perfume, electronic equipment, candy, ethnic foods. . . . It was loud and garish and gaudy. After the narrow, quaint, one-way streets of the West Village, the three-story old brick buildings, the charming little pastry shops and antiques stores, Fourteenth Street was like a big, startling slap on the back.

What was she doing here? Gaia faltered on the street corner, mesmerized by the four lanes of traffic speeding past her. How easy it would be to step out into it. It would all be over in moments, her whole, stupid, messy, pointless life. She probably wouldn't feel a thing.

The light changed, and still Gaia remained, standing on a corner next to a trash can. Behind her was a subway stop for the F and the L trains. She felt their rumble beneath her feet. She looked down. There was blood on the toe of her boot.

Oh my God, what am I going to do? Her friendship with Mary and Ed had seemed to give her life a little structure, purpose. They had cared about her. They had been teaching her how to care about them. As if she could have a normal life. Then Mary had died. In the end, Mary's seventeen years of life, from birth, through school, through family holidays, through adolescence, had been worth five hundred bucks.

Revenge against Skizz had been the only thing keeping her going for the past week. It had been the only goal she could wrap her mind around. She had hoped the pain would stop with his death. She'd never figured on someone beating her to him.

Now what was she going to do with herself? Years of her life stretched before her like some arid chasm, like thousands of miles of desert with no water, no other people in sight. Really, what was the point? Shaking her head, Gaia acknowledged that there *was* no point. There was no purpose in her going any further with this. This charade of an existence.

Yes. Just a few quick steps into the street . . .

ED SAW GAIA STANDING ON THE STREET

Cream Puff

corner, looking pensive. With a last burst of energy he rolled right up into her, knocking hard against her hip. She winced and sucked in breath.

"What the hell do you think you're doing?" Ed yelled at her. His brown eyes were narrowed, his hair and face damp with sweat. Cheeks flushed, he was still blowing hard with the effort of following her for block after block, catching up with her.

Gaia turned, anger coloring her cheeks and making her blue eyes ignite. "Why do you always have to interfere?" she asked snidely.

Ed pushed his sweaty hair back off his forehead with an impatient gesture. "Yeah, you're bummed. Skizz is dead, and you didn't get a chance to kill him. You're disappointed!" he spat. "You're disappointed you didn't get to make the stupidest mistake of your life!" He saw her eyes flare open.

"You're disappointed you didn't get to destroy *yourself* along with destroying *him*. You stupid *idiot!* You would have ended up in jail, no better than any other lowlife murderer! Is that what you wanted? You stupid *bitch!*" he shouted, enraged.

Gaia stared at him in horror. "Go screw yourself," she choked out. She moved quickly to the side, obviously intending to lose him.

Quickly, without thinking, Ed spun sideways as well, making Gaia literally trip over his left wheel.

"Oof!" She sprawled gracelessly on the filthy sidewalk in front of him. "You shit," she hissed. "Get out of my way."

"Make me," he taunted. "I'll get out of your way when you promise to go to Mary's funeral. That'll show me you're not completely hopeless. That'll show me you still have some human quality in you."

"When hell freezes over!" Scrambling to her feet, Gaia backed away from Ed carefully, but he pursued her.

"If you're not getting the message, leave me alone!" Gaia snarled.

"Make me," Ed said again.

In the short course of their relationship Ed had never pushed her this far. In any dispute he was always the one to back down, the one who tried to make up, the one who placated. Those days were over.

"What is *wrong* with you?" she said, eyes narrowed. She was still backing away from him, and over her right shoulder Ed caught sight of a subway sign. So that was her plan. She knew most subways were Ed-proof. He had to accomplish his mission fast.

"No, no," Ed murmured with deadly calm, his brown eyes locked on hers. He was still breathing hard, but he ratcheted down his voice. "The question is, what's wrong with *you*? You had exactly two friends in this world, which isn't a surprise, considering what a cold, insensitive *bitch* you like to pretend you are."

Gaia's eyes flickered. He reloaded and kept firing at her.

"You had two friends," Ed continued, rolling slowly toward her as she backed away. "One of them died a stupid, tragic death. But you know what? Here's a life lesson for you. The life lesson is that even though you lose one friend, it doesn't mean you need to lose *all* your friends. It doesn't mean you can't make new friends in the future. Hasn't anyone ever told you that?"

Gaia made a cruel, mocking face. "Ed, eat shit and die," she said conversationally. "You don't know the first thing about me. You don't know what you're talking about."

Ed felt his face contort again in anger, and he jerked his wheels, making his chair surge forward. He let his metal footrests whack Gaia's shins painfully, and she shoved at him. He held his wheels in place. She whirled and sprang for the subway opening. He watched almost in amusement as she realized that she didn't have a token handy to get through the turnstile. But a train had just pulled out, and people were streaming through the swing gate to one side. Gaia darted through, edging past people: totally illegal.

Two can play at that game, Ed thought, wheeling quickly forward. Ahead of him Gaia looked back, crashing into a young gang banger as Ed pushed himself through the gate. Then Ed was on Gaia again, at the top of a cement stair that led down to the train platform. The air, only feet from the opening, was dank, chill, and smelled of urine and steam.

"You're wrong," he spat out, coming to within a foot of her. "I *do* know the first thing about you. I know you're a self-centered *asshole*. This whole thing with Skizz wasn't even about Mary! It was all about *you! Your* ego, *your* feelings, *your* pain. You weren't helping Mary by hunting Skizz—you were helping only yourself." His jaw was clenched so tightly, it almost hurt to talk. "You're not in charge of fixing the world, you know? You're just one person. Give it a rest!"

Gaia stared at Ed, a tiny muscle under her left eye twitching. He could practically feel the white-hot anger and hatred coming off her. It was like losing a friend all over again, and it made him unbearably sad. But not as sad as the thought of Gaia, beautiful, special Gaia, going through life so totally screwed up.

"Roll on home, loser," she said softly.

"Bite me," he offered. He shook his head. "You think you're so tough," he said. As he spoke, his voice rose in volume and intensity until he was shouting again, so loudly that veins stood out in his neck. "You are such a deluded *coward*. Tough Gaia. No one touches her. She doesn't care about anyone. She's a freaking icicle. But *I* know the truth, even if you don't. I know you're a *cream puff!* I know you're hurt about Mary and lonely without *me*. I know you're scared to go to Mary's funeral. You stupid, stupid ass-hole!" he yelled. "You don't even know how much you love me!"

Gaia stepped back, but Ed wasn't finished. He was more enraged than he'd ever been in his whole life. He saw Gaia force her face into a controlled mask and knew if she said another flippant remark, he'd never forgive her. Without warning his fist swept out and smacked her across the face, hard. Her head snapped sideways, and she staggered, just for a moment.

TIME ALMOST SEEMED TO STOP IN

Torn Apart

the first few seconds after Ed had hit her. It was funny, Gaia thought dully, holding her hand to her cheek. She had been in more fights than most heavyweights, and this was the first time she actually had felt pain on contact. Slowly she straightened and looked across at Ed. He looked as shocked as she felt, and in his transparent, dark brown eyes she could read regret, fury, love, and a terrible sadness.

She swallowed hard. Here she'd been so proud of herself for successfully holding herself immune from friendship. Now Skizz was dead; she had no friends, no parents, no nothing. She had been sure she could control the pain, but her hip was killing her, her cheek felt like it was on fire, and her emotions felt like Ed had rolled them through broken glass and then sprayed her with water from the Dead Sea.

I simply cannot stand this, Gaia thought in the last, silent moment before she pulled back her right arm, swung it in a huge, lightning-fast arc, and gave Ed a powerful punch right across his kisser.

His eyes had just time enough to register surprise before his chair jerked backward and began to fall down the long, scarred cement steps toward the train platform. Ed's strong arms scrambled for his wheels, and for a second he managed to keep himself upright, but Gaia could see it was only a matter of moments before he tilted backward and crashed down the steps, probably breaking his neck and paralyzing the *rest* of him.

Without wasting time on thought, Gaia lunged

after Ed and scrabbled for his jacket, his arm, anything. She missed, and he continued to slide backward, now on the third step, now on the fourth. His angle of descent was increasing as his chair leaned farther and farther back. The distant roar of an incoming train grew louder.

Again Gaia lunged at him, her fingers brushing against his shoe. His wide, frightened eyes locked on hers, but Gaia saw no blame in them—only fear. That odd, familiar emotion that she recognized so easily in others, yet never felt herself.

Curiously, neither of them made a sound: Ed didn't cry out for help; Gaia didn't call his name. A gust of stale air announced that the train was about to reach the station.

With a last surge Gaia plunged heedlessly down the steps, throwing herself at Ed. Her bloodied glove snatched at Ed's jacket lapel and held it in an iron grip. With one arm she gave a powerful yank and managed to haul him forward. His wheelchair, freed of its weight, bounced crazily down the remaining steps, gathering momentum. It sprang across the narrow platform and smashed into the front of an express train, steaming through the station on its way to Twenty-third Street. The chair popped up high, seemingly weightless, then crashed down again on the roof of the train's third car. The train's speed ricocheted the chair off the track, and it came to rest on the platform twenty feet away. It was mangled, the size of an electric can opener.

Ed's ripstop nylon saddlebag, shredded, now consisted of a torn canvas strap and some threads. All of his painstaking class notes were floating through the air like ungainly, oversized snowflakes. They littered the platform, landing on passengers, on the train tracks, on Ed and Gaia.

The noise of the train faded—it hadn't even slowed down. The few people coming down the steps simply passed around Gaia and Ed, clutching each other halfway down the stairs. The scene would need to be much more unusual to merit attention.

Gaia swallowed, clutching Ed. Slowly he braced his arms on the steps and eased himself upward to sit next to her on the step. She didn't release her hold to make it easier for him. She felt like she could never let him go again. She stared into his eyes, and he returned the look.

"You still have my handprint on your cheek," he said in a shaky voice.

"You still have mine on yours," she told him, her voice warbling stupidly. The enormity of what had almost happened tried to filter into her brain, but she resisted it.

Ed gave her a crooked grin, though his face was still white with shock, almost greenish around the edges. "Love pats," he said.

Gaia had the sudden certainty that she was going to throw up. Emotion was rising painfully through her chest, and it was terrifying and nauseating. *Oh God.*

"I almost lost you," she blurted out, unable to articulate the kind of disaster she knew his loss would be. Having lost Mary, she now realized that losing Ed would be unbearable. It was as if a stained glass window had shattered inside her mind, showing her the white light of her feelings, her connection to Ed, her best friend. "Ed," she muttered, overwhelmed. "Oh God." Now she was trembling more than he was, and she felt his arms come around her strongly, reassuringly.

"Tell me you love me," Ed said softly.

The thought *I would rather be torn apart by wild animals* crossed her mind, but she shoved it down. This was the test. If she passed this test, she could choose life. If she didn't pass this test, she might as well have thrown herself into the traffic ten minutes before.

Oh God. Help.

She couldn't look at him. "I love you." Her voice cracked, and she gave a wet little cough. Ed's arms tightened around her.

"I love you, too," he said back, and kissed her hair. Then she started to cry.

Gaia had
come through
the
fire **courage**
and emerged
tempered,
not charred.

GAIA FROWNED. "WHAT IS THAT?"

Ed, looking surprisingly presentable in a navy blazer, white shirt, and tie, rolled up to her at the handicapped entrance of the Riverside Chapel. The thin, Wednesday morning light barely dusted his shoulders and glinted off the wheels of a clunky, old-fashioned wheelchair.

 **Enough Chitcha**

"Rental," Ed answered glumly. Then his face brightened. "But the 'rents ordered me a new one. A racer."

"Good. You needed a style update. Your last chair was so 1999." Gaia pulled her jacket more tightly around her.

"Yeah. Is that enough chitchat?" Ed asked.

"Yes, I think so," Gaia replied reluctantly.

"Then let's hit it."

And they went into the chapel to attend Mary Moss's funeral.

THE MOSSES, BOTH PARENTS AND

Mary's three siblings, sat in the first row of the small chapel. Other relatives took up the next four rows.

We Remembe You

Ed and Gaia sat together in the fifth row, with Ed's rental chair practically blocking the aisle. He moved backward a few inches to let Gaia out when it was time for her to speak.

Obviously uncomfortable but moving with her innate grace, Gaia climbed the two steps to the podium to the right of the altar. She tapped the microphone experimentally and sent a buzz through the room. Ed winced, then quickly smoothed his face into what he hoped looked like supportive expectation.

With her repulsive jacket stuffed under the pew, Gaia looked pretty close to presentable. She wore some sort of dark skirt thing, with a thin, pale blue sweater on top. No jewelry flashed under the lights, but she had actually brushed her hair this morning, and it hung in clean, soft, golden waves down her back. She was gorgeous.

"Ahem. I, uh, just wanted to say a few words about my friend Mary. Who we're all here to remember today. On this . . . sad day." Gaia drew in a deep breath.

"Actually, I only knew Mary a really short time. But she made an impression on me that very few other people have made." She looked out into the chapel and met Ed's eyes.

"Mary was an incredibly strong person," Gaia went on. "She was incredibly brave. Most people can't face their problems, their faults." She looked down. "But Mary could and did. And she beat them. She showed me it was possible to do if you have courage."

In the front row Mrs. Moss gazed up at Gaia, her eyes brimming with unshed tears. Gaia tried not to look at her again.

"Not only that, but Mary showed me how to have fun. How to enjoy life. How to work with what you have and do the best with it. We had some great times together." Gaia swallowed. "Times I'll remember the rest of my life. And she showed me something else: how to *be* a friend. How to have a friend. What it feels like when someone cares about you." Looking right at Ed, Gaia said, "Those were lessons I wasn't ready to learn before. But I'd like to thank Mary now for teaching them to me." Her voice wobbled, and Gaia frowned and cleared her throat. Then she looked out at the group.

"Now Mary is going to continue in our memories," Gaia said. "I hope you all have good memories of her, as I do. I remember her laugh, her crazy red hair, her daring fashion sense." Some people in the audience smiled. "But I don't really need to remember Mary on purpose. Because every time I actually manage to be a friend to someone or let them be my friend, I'll know that Mary is right there with me."

Not knowing how to end or if she should say thank you or what, Gaia simply stopped speaking and stepped down from the podium. As she passed the first row, Mr. and Mrs. Moss smiled at her. "Thank you," whispered Mrs. Moss. Gaia nodded at her.

Safely back in her own seat, Gaia felt breathless, as if

she had just run a hundred blocks. The minister stood up in the front of the chapel and started speaking, but Gaia couldn't concentrate on what he was saying.

Ed reached across the arm of the pew and took Gaia's hand. Without looking at him, she squeezed back and held on.

To: L 43671.1011@alloymail.com
From: ELJ 239.211@alloymail.com

Subject was observed at memorial service sitting with young male. They were observed holding hands. Later, subject was observed wiping away tears with sleeve of sweater. Young male subject (in wheelchair) hugged her. She did not resist.

IN THE BACK OF THE CHAPEL TOM

Something of Katia

Moore turned up the collar of his coat. Something in his chest tightened when he saw the golden head of his daughter lean against the shoulder of the young man in the wheelchair.

Gaia had gone to Mary Moss's funeral. Gaia and her handicapped friend had apparently made up. Gaia had been seen to cry, to lean on someone, again.

An overwhelming sense of joy and relief flooded Tom. This past week his guts had been almost chewed out by his worry about his daughter. His unfeeling, automaton-like daughter. His daughter whose emotions had effectively been destroyed, whose sense of loyalty, of compassion, of humanity had been obliterated, surely and effectively, by decisions he alone had made.

Who knew what would have happened if she had actually been the one to kill Skizz? Tom winced at the thought. Gaia was capable of great courage. But she was also capable of great rage. It had been the right decision to take Skizz out of the equation. A difficult decision, but the right one.

But there was no use dwelling on that. Gaia had come through the fire and emerged tempered, not charred. It was more than Tom had hoped for. It was more than he deserved.

As he stood and made his way quietly to the chapel door, Tom Moore gave thanks that his daughter had some remnants of her mother still existing with her. Katia lived on, in Gaia. And for that Tom was grateful.

here is a sneak peek of Fearless™ #10: LIAR

Here I am, at my desk trying to do my English homework like a normal seventeen-year-old girl on a normal Friday afternoon. But the problem is I can't get past the opening sentence of this book, *The Great Gatsby*. In fact, I keep reading it over and over again. I know it sounds a little psychotic. But I can't stop.

"In my younger and more vulnerable years my father gave me some advice that I've been turning over in my mind ever since."

That's the sentence.

It's like the author, this Fitzgerald guy, is winking at me through the pages or something. "Father" and "advice" are not words I tend to use in close proximity to one another— definitely not in the same sentence.

See, my father hasn't blessed me with any wisdom in quite some time. Not since he went MIA five

years ago. Not since I got stuck
in foster care and bounced from
one crappy home to the next until
I ended up in Greenwich Village
with a sweet but entirely clueless old agency buddy of my
dad's, George Niven, and his
wretched wife Ella, the hoochie
housefrau.

And no, in case you're wondering, George and Ella are not what
you'd call parental figures. We
have an understanding. They don't
pretend to be my parents, and I
don't pretend to need any. I
mean, they don't ask me to turn
over my report card or turn down
the music or return home by midnight—let alone ever ask me if I
could use any advice.

So, anyway. Father. Advice.
These are two of the things I'm
missing. Not to mention a mother.
A home. Fear. Mary. A boyfriend.
The list goes on and on.

The thing is, I could definitely use some advice right now.
Especially about Sam. There are

just so many questions. Like why did he literally run away from my house as soon as he saw Ella on New Years Eve? What was that about? Why didn't he ever call or e-mail to explain what happened that night?

You'd think I could ask a friend for advice, but I only have one of those. His name is Ed and he tenses up at the mention of Sam. Mary would have given me advice about Sam. She would have known exactly what to do—whether to call or not to call, or e-mail him. Whether to casually bump into him at the chess tables in the park. How to apologize for acting like a sociopath when I ran into him at the library. Mary would have been able to advise me, but she is gone. You'd think I'd get used to missing things and that it wouldn't have to hurt so much anymore.

But there you have it. No advice for Gaia. No one to talk to about why it is that I'm per-

fectly cool in the face of thugs,
drug dealers, rapists, muggers,
knives, and firearms, but an awkward, stammering moron around
Sam.

Wait. So where was I? Oh,
yeah. I was sitting here at my
desk trying to act like a normal
seventeen-year-old girl, trying
to do her homework on a normal
Friday afternoon. Trying to imagine what it would be like to have
a little good advice. And maybe
more than that, trying to imagine
what it would be like to still
have a dad who could give it.

Sam could hardly
stop himself
from running
after Gaia, from
screaming her
name at **almost**
the top of his
lungs. From
telling her how
beautiful
she was.

"CRUELLA DE VILLE, EAT YOUR

heart out," Gaia muttered under her breath as she watched Ella Niven wrap herself in an utterly atrocious floor-length leopard print coat.

Cruella

"What was that?" Ella asked.

"Don't worry about it," Gaia said, reaching into the hall closet to grab her blue down jacket off a hanger. It was almost 3:30 P.M., which meant she was almost late to meet Ed. The last thing she needed right now was to get into some pointless altercation with The Bimbo.

But perhaps it was already too late. Gaia felt Ella's glare on her back.

"And where are you off to, Miss Moore?" Ella inquired icily, moving in front of the door.

"*Excuse* me?" Gaia nearly laughed. Ella *had* to be kidding. Like she had any right to track Gaia's comings and goings.

But Ella, not amused, asked again, this time as slowly as if she were speaking to a mentally challenged five-year-old, "Where . . . are . . . you . . . GOING?"

"Tell you what, Ella," Gaia challenged, a glint in her eye. "You tell me where you're going . . . and I'll tell you."

Gaia *was* actually pretty curious to know where Ella was slipping off to in that long coat and minuscule skirt. What was her deal? Was she fooling around behind George's back? Living a double life? Did she

6

have another poor sucker like George hidden uptown or something?

Ella scowled at Gaia, but remained silent.

"Hmmmm. Thought so," Gaia said, victorious. "So why don't we just stick to our little don't ask don't tell policy? It seems to be working pretty well so far, don't you think?"

And, with that, Gaia blew her way past Ella, slamming the door behind her for effect.

SAM LOOKED AT HIS G-SHOCK AND

Black Ice

exhaled deeply, watching his breath billow in the frigid February air. He'd been freezing his ass off in the alley by Gaia's brownstone for almost half an hour, and he was beginning to lose feeling in his toes. Stomping his Timberlands on the pavement to defrost his feet, he slid sideways, nearly wiping out before steadying himself with the help of a nearby fire escape.

Damn, Sam, thought, looking down. *Black ice.*

That's what he was standing on. A slippery film. Smooth. Clear. Invisible. Sam decided he'd take regular ice any day. You know, the white, or slightly grayish, thick, bumpy kind? The kind that let you know it was there. The kind that cried out to be skated on or sanded or salted or shoveled away. Or avoided altogether. Black ice, though, was insidious. It deceived you.

Deception, Sam had quickly learned, was not a game he could play. In fact, everything in his life had gone from bad to worse the night he deceived Heather. The night he cheated. How could he have been so stupid? How could he have made such a horrendous error in judgment? He'd drunk too much and slept with a stunningly seductive redhead. He knew the woman was a little older, but he sure as hell never could have guessed she was Gaia's hated foster mother. It still seemed so unbelievable. Like some cruel joke. He'd literally freaked out on New Year's when he put it together. That Ella was Gaia's guardian. It was a twist of fate too twisted to imagine.

It was this nauseating coincidence that led Sam to the alley adjacent to Gaia's brownstone this particular Friday afternoon. He was waiting for Ella to emerge from the house. He was waiting to confront her. To explain that the night they spent together was a monumental mistake. A mistake that under no circumstances could ever or would ever be repeated. A mistake that Gaia could never, ever, *ever* know about.

An NYPD cruiser rounded the corner and slowed down, interrupting Sam's train of thought. Sam watched in mild amusement as the two members of New York City's finest gave him, a collegiate kid in a

Rangers cap and camel hair coat, a once-over. Did he look like a stalker or something? Apparently not. The cops sped away before Sam could even blink. He had to smile. He was an unlikely criminal. He looked a lot more like Holden Caulfield than Hannibal Lechter.

Yeah, sure, he was staking out the Nivens' home. But *he* wasn't the stalker. Ella was. She was stalking him with e-mails and calls. He was there to insist that she stop. To issue his own version of, what do they call it? A restraining order. That was it. He was going to demand that Ella leave him alone—forever.

Yes. Sam was going to set everything straight. He was tired of waffling and wavering, of dating Heather but desiring Gaia. It was time to make some decisions. To go after what he wanted. To follow his heart.

Collision Course

SAM'S HEART NEARLY STOPPED. THE front door of the brownstone had finally swung open. But it was not Ella Niven who appeared.

It was Gaia Moore. Gaia bounding down the steps. Gaia zipping up her jacket. Gaia slipping her slender fingers into a pair of torn gloves. Gaia freeing her long hair from the collar of her jacket, letting it stream behind her.

He knew it was trite and completely shallow, but Gaia looked like, well . . . like a model. Not in a fashion-victim-waif sort of a way. No, Gaia would definitely be the healthy, outdoorsy, sporty kind of model. In fact, in that ski jacket and jeans, Sam half expected Gaia to pick up a snowball and playfully throw it at some hunky snowboarder who just happened to be wandering by. He could see the description:

ON HER: *Pleasantly puffy down-filled parka. Shown here in Beaver Creek Blue. Also available in Aspen Azure, Vail Violet, and Telluride Teal.*

ON HIM: *Seventeen-pocket Polar fleece vest. In Periwinkle. One size fits all.*

The thing was, Gaia seemed to have no idea. That quality of hers was as striking as her face. Generally speaking, girls in Manhattan tended to *know* they were hot. It was like a full-time job. They strutted down Prince Street in the latest trends looking like they knew they were being checked out by every passerby—male and female. They breezed past velvet ropes at the hippest clubs, charming the bouncers who opened doors and the businessmen who bought them champagne. They were self-possessed and perfectly put together. Girls like Heather, actually.

But Gaia. Gaia was different. Gaia was refreshing. Gaia had no idea. She had no idea, for example, how stunning she looked at this very moment as she swiftly strode toward Washington Square Park. That leggy gait. That glowing blond mane floating behind her. . . .

Instead, the front door swung open again and Sam snapped back to reality. This time it *was* Ella. She paused on the steps of the brownstone distracted by a ringing sound. Sam watched as Ella fished through her pocketbook, and finding what she was looking for, flipped open her cell phone and began walking briskly down the block.

Sam glanced one last time back at Gaia. The sight gave him courage. Taking a deep breath, he headed after Ella.

Ella, consumed in conversation, didn't seem to hear Sam's footsteps behind her. Sam, however, could hear Ella. She was arguing animatedly with someone on the other end of the line.

"*I'm* talking about the dead girl, too. And I'm telling you any action taken was completely necessary," Ella told the caller.

Dead girl? Necessary? What the hell was Ella talking

about? Sam felt a chill crawling up his legs, and it wasn't only frostbite.

Instinctively he drew closer. Ella dropped her voice, but only a little.

So her parents are rich. Who cares? There are plenty of rich people in New York City. They don't all have influence with The Agency. What do you think they are going to do? Call Hillary Clinton?

Sam's head was spinning. No coincidence was too great or too terrifying when it came to Ella. It was almost as if she was talking about . . .

"Moss," Ella hissed. "You *knew* that."

Mary Moss. God, was Ella really saying this stuff? Did it mean what it sounded like it meant? Was Ella involved in Mary's death? Oh God.

The chill had numbed his spine and shoulders. What had he gotten himself into? This thing with Ella was sicker and scarier than anything he'd conceived of. What should he do? Follow Ella? Find Gaia and tell her what he'd heard? Go to the police?

Ella stepped off the curb and extended her arm to hail a cab.

Sam followed her into the street.

Deep breath. Deep breath, he ordered himself. Think. Think. Think fast.

Sam stood there frozen. Should he follow Ella? Or maybe go after Gaia. He knew he had to warn her, even if it meant telling her the truth.

But Sam did neither. He just stood there in the middle of the street, not noticing the sound of a car starting up behind him or the screech of its tires as it lurched into the street. It was only the loud long wail of the car's horn that made Sam finally turn and see a brown Lexus taking off at top speed after the taxi— and headed right for him.

It was like one of those slow-motion moments in a movie. When all the sound drains out, except for the unnaturally loud thumping of the hero's beating heart.

Right now, Sam thought numbly, *I should probably be seeing my life flashing before my eyes.*

Wasn't that what was supposed to happen when you were about to die? But instead, Sam's mind was blank. There he was, in the middle of the street. His feet wouldn't move. Couldn't move. And, all he knew was that it was too late. He was going to be hit by a car. He was a goner.

TOM MOORE PULLED HIS BROWN LEXUS away from the corner of **Brake** Seventh Avenue and West Fourth Street and followed the cab Ella had stepped into moments before. The afternoon sun bounced off the windshield and into his eyes, making him squint as he hurried to catch up.

As he sped past the spot where Ella had stepped into the taxi, Tom noticed his daughter walking on the sidewalk, holding a blue jacket closed tightly against the freezing wind as she made her way through skateboarders and street vendors.

And that's when he saw the kid. Or the back of the kid, really. Just standing there in the middle of the street. Definitely not seeing the Lexus speeding toward him. Definitely not getting out of the way.

Tom hit the horn hard. The kid spun around, his eyes open wide in fear. He looked familiar, this kid. Did Tom know him? Was it . . . ? There was no time to think. Tom slammed both feet on the brakes, closing his eyes.

When he opened them it was Gaia, not the kid that Tom saw sprinting from the sidewalk into the intersection, hurdling garbage cans and parking meters, her hair flying loose and whipping wildly behind her.

What was she doing? Trying to save this kid? Tom's mind reeled. It was all happening way too fast. Desperate, Tom pulled on the emergency brake, sending the Lexus into a violent spin.

From inside the spinning car, the rest of the world suddenly appeared to Tom with amazing clarity. He could see Gaia diving into the traffic unafraid, arcing her back over and across the speeding car like a high-

14

jumper. He could see the look of recognition and disbelief on the kid's face, as she pushed him to safety. And then the expression of complete surprise, wonder almost, on his daughter's face, as the brown Lexus slammed right into her.

He watched Gaia's body fly high up into the air and then crash down hard onto the hood of the car, as it careened to a stop. Oh, Jesus.

His heart was flooded with relief when Gaia picked up her head. She was alive. For a split second she seemed to look right at Tom. Then just as quickly she looked away and rolled off the hood of the car to safety with the grace of a cat.

Thank God the car had slowed by the time he'd struck her. Thank God she appeared to be all right. She appeared to be all right, but he couldn't be sure.

He threw the Lexus into reverse and dialed three numbers into his car phone. A voice answered:

"911 emergency."

"I'd like to report a hit-and-run at the corner of West Fourth and Seventh Avenue," he said, as he sped away from the intersection. "You better call an ambulance."

"And your name, Sir?" the operator asked.

The line went dead silent. Tom was long gone.

Buffy
the Vampire Slayer™

"Well, we could grind our enemies into powder with a sledgehammer, but gosh, we did that last night."

—Xander

As long as there have been vampires, there has been the Slayer. One girl in all the world, to find them where they gather and to stop the spread of their evil...the swell of their numbers.

LOOK FOR A NEW TITLE EVERY MONTH!

Based on the hit TV series created by
Joss Whedon

Everyone's got his demons....

ANGEL™

If it takes an eternity, he will make amends.

❖

Original stories based
on the TV show
Created by Joss Whedon
& David Greenwalt

Available from Simon Pulse
Published by Simon & Schuster

SIMON
PULSE

2311-01